I0779143

Cash Pawley

Pray for Death

Inspired By True Events

THE FLYING TIGERS
PUBLISHING GROUP

Pray For Death

Pray For Death

This is a work of fiction. Although inspired by real events, most of the events described are imaginary, the characters areentirely fictitious and are not intended to represent actual living persons.

THE FLYING TIGERS PUBLISHING GROUP EDITION

Copyright © 2004 by *Cash Pawley*
All rights reserved
www.cashpawley.com

Cover design by Cash Pawley
All graphics and photos used with permission

LIBRARY OF CONGRESS
CATALOGING-IN-PUBLICATION DATA
has been applied for.

ISBN: 1438218834

EAN-13: 978-0-615-15794-8

Printed in the United States of America

1ˢᵗ Hardcover Edition printed in arrangement with
Lulu.com: 2007

Without limiting the rights under the copyright above, no part of this publication may be reproduced, stored in or introduced into a retrieval system, or transmitted, in any form, or by any means (electronic, mechanical, photocopying, recording, or otherwise), without the prior written consent of both the copyright owner and the above publisher of this book.

Pray For Death

DEDICATION:

To Amber and Joel...

Without whom this book would have never made it to print.

Pray For Death

PRELUDE

A glint of light, from the ritualistic array of candles in the room, shown off the smooth edge of the long, pearl handled razor blade as it effortlessly sliced away her beauty. Tears streamed down her face from her terror filled eyes. Her body jerked and squirmed like a night crawler pinched between a fisherman's fingers, only to make her restraints tighten down harder, cutting harshly into her wrists and ankles. Sweat and fear pumped from every pore on her body. Her nakedness was exposed as she laid face up, legs spread wide, on the black satin sheets that covered her bed. There was no pain - at first, just a small initial tug, then a tiny sting, followed by the sensation of warm blood trickling over her mound and down between her buttocks. She tried to scream over Type O Negative's - *'Love You to Death'* blaring on the radio, but her voice was too hoarse from the numerous other attempts over the last hour. This was how long she had been gagged and bound to the head and footboards of the solid, cherry wood, sleigh bed. Her eyes pressed closed for a few seconds, only to reopen to a complete blur. They were burning now from her salty tears. She managed to see the outline of her attacker as he methodically stitched up her wounds.

Suddenly, everything went black...

Pray For Death

~ 1 ~

- Four Weeks Earlier -

The beginning of October is interesting in the mountains of Western North Carolina. Summer is now over, and school buses have taken the place of ice cream trucks on the winding mountainous roads.
The leaves have turned yellow and golden brown, and litter the streets of seemingly otherwise pristine neighborhoods. Tourists are now setting off the familiar 'cha-chings' of cash registers throughout the region.
Asheville is a small city nestled snugly in the Great Smokey Mountains, in the far southwestern corner of the state. It's hardly large enough to actually be called a 'city', but slightly larger in population than most of the surrounding towns. It's a unique city, with the medical field being its biggest occupational trade, a Wiccan Witch for a Mayor, more corrupt police and politicians than Washington D.C., and a fairly new reputation as the 'Lesbian Capital of the World'.
Downtown Asheville, despite its pleasant facade, attracts folks from all walks of life. During the day, the streets are littered with college students, tourists, lower-middle classed transients, and a sea of 'Tree Huggers' - or as the

locals call them… 'Earth Biscuits'. As nighttime falls, the city is transformed into a beautifully landscaped flow of downtown nightclubs, street side cafes and coffee houses, surrounded by the usual drug dealers, prostitutes and 'nare-do-wells' that plague most cities. The suburbs, however, offer up a different lifestyle, depending on which direction you decide to venture.

To the North: Upper classed retirees ride around slowly in their late model Buicks without a care in the world - seeming almost oblivious to their surroundings.

The Southern end of town is made up mainly of professional individuals and families, mostly in their 20's and early 30's. It's a congregation of Firemen, Policemen, Mechanics, lower end Medical Field workers, Car Salesmen, Restaurant Managers and similar 'working class' folks.

The East side of town is about a ten mile stretch of mobile home parks, separated by the occasional fast food restaurant and dumpy strip mall centers, until you reach the wonderfully quaint town of Black Mountain. The Veteran's Hospital, in all its eyesore-splendor, stands eerily, about halfway between the two points.

Finally, the West is an area most desirable to middle classed transplants. Rent is fairly cheap, and the property sizes are considerably larger than other areas. It gives people a bit more 'breathing room' - for those that it makes a difference to. People from all over the country seem to flock to this area between Asheville - in Buncombe County, and the neighboring Haywood County. Buncombe County, in general, is a melting pot of all walks of life - once you include the vast array of Doctors, Lawyers, Business Owners and other wealthy and super wealthy citizens that speckle the population.

Pray For Death

~ 2 ~

The aroma of sizzling bacon and good ole' southern biscuits and gravy filled the air outside Jackie's - the local diner in Leicester, a small mostly farming community just outside Asheville's city limits. The diner is a small nondescript place that seats forty people at most, open only for breakfast and an early lunch. Getting a seat during the week, in the A.M. hours, would best be compared to getting a dinner seating at the World Famous 'Joe's Stone Crabs' in Miami Beach, Florida - in high season… Virtually Impossible! However, one table always remained available in the far rear corner, next to the antiquated wood-burning heater. Just arriving to fill that table, like clockwork at 7 a.m. sharp, was the County Sheriff - Jimmy 'Buster' Cagle, and his entourage of three local Deputies - each one arriving in their own patrol car.

Leicester, while being a small close-knit community where everybody knows each other, was still close enough to Asheville to warrant its own share of community crime. Especially since the only topless bar in town, Diamonds Adult Entertainment had opened there just a year earlier. Buster, as the locals called him, was a rather large man framed at 6'4" and 260 pounds. At fifty, he had a soft, hairless, cherub type face with a cockeyed smile and his lower lip was always sporting a permanent bulge of Skoal. His wife of twenty-nine years, Betty Joe, had made him give up smoking five years ago, but now wasn't sure which she hated worse - the smoke or the worm dirt.

"Mornin' Buster, Mornin' Boys," echoed out from a few different tables full of locals in their overalls, work boots and John Deer caps.

Making his way to his table, Buster bellowed a greeting back at each of them. The three Deputies, sunglasses all still firmly on their faces, simply nodded their greetings without even a smile. They all sat down in one seemingly choreographed move. The one waitress in the house poured them all some coffee and took their orders. The table was completely silent until their food arrived a few minutes later.

"Busta'," blurted one of the Deputies, "anything new we needs ta' know about on the slice-em' dice-em' case?"

"Damnit Willy!" belted the Sheriff. "How many times do I have to tell you not to refer to it that way? It's bad enough the damn tabloids have exploited it that way. We don't need to fuel that fire around town."

"Sorry Boss. Didn't mean nottin' by it."

"Just eat your eggs Willy," the Sheriff replied.

Willy Biddle was a former porta-jon deliveryman, and now second year rookie with the Buncombe County Sheriff's Office. He was what many would say, 'a hamburger short of a Happy Meal'. At twenty-three, he stood all of 5'7" and weighed not an ounce more than 135lbs - soaking wet. Being that Willy was black, had virtually guaranteed his acceptance to the force under county quota requirements.
"Well, is there anything new Buster?" another Deputy asked hesitantly.

"No goddamnit, no!" Buster raged. He threw down a fork onto his plate, sending gravy splattering. "I'm going to work now," he bellowed as he stood up and threw his napkin onto the table. He grabbed his Stetson hat and strolled aggressively towards the door. As he passed the cash register by the front door, he tossed a five dollar bill on top of it and bolted outside.

Buster Cagle was all too familiar with the 'slice- em' dice-em' case. He had initially assigned Steve Layton, his Sex Crimes Detective, to the case after the first attack. However, when a second attack occurred, he knew that public pressure would force him to assign another Detective to the case. Ken Barton, from Homicide, would be that man. Although there were no murders in this case, the County was not large enough to have two Detectives permanently working in their Sexual Crimes Division. The Sheriff had been left with no other choice, as he would never have asked the S.B.I. (State Bureau of Investigation) for their assistance. This would have made the County look incompetent to the Press, and ultimately to the constituents that would hopefully reelect him as Sheriff next month.

~ 3 ~

It had been a distressing scene two weeks earlier when Detective Layton had arrived at the well kept, single wide trailer in Swannanoa to investigate the first attack. As he had approached the front door, yellow police tape was already x'd across it. An EMT suddenly pushed up on the tape as he hurriedly pulled a gurney behind him - another EMT in tow at the other end. A uniformed police officer held an IV bag as they frantically came down the rickety steps and shot across the lawn to the awaiting ambulance. On the gurney was a woman, or at least he assumed it was, by the way the sheet draped over her more than average sized breasts. He could not see her face, as it was heavily wrapped in bloodied gauze from forehead to chin. A slightly mortified, yet puzzled look came across the Detective's face as the stretcher passed him on the lawn. He turned and flashed his badge at another officer guarding the doorway, stooped under the tape and entered the trailer.

The scene inside was slightly less than gruesome. Blood was draped all over the living room walls, but it was in thin streaks, and almost artistically placed. It looked as though it was splattered intentionally by a fairly small paintbrush. Similar streaks also covered selective furniture around the room, from lamps to drapes. The only person in the room was a Forensic Investigator, snapping photographs from a multitude of angles. Peering down a short hallway to his right, the Detective noticed a half opened doorway at the end. He took a few steps towards the doorway, pushed the door farther open and sidestepped his way in. He immediately noticed a queen-sized bed almost perfectly centered along the far wall of the room. From where he was now standing, he could see three of the bed's legs. To each was tied what looked like thin straight telephone cords. The remainder of the cords casually draped across the floor, each about two and a half feet in length. Each one had been cut at the other ends, presumably by whoever had discovered the victim tied to the bed. The sheets were tussled a bit, but not quite in disarray.

Layton cautiously stepped closer to the bed, so as not to disturb anything in the room. As he approached, he noticed the bedcovers were not your usual run of the mill cotton blend. They were a sleek, silvery satin - and they were drenched in blood.

As the Detective looked at the blood a little closer, he slid his hands into a pair of surgical gloves. He bent over the bed as if looking down the shaft of an old water well. His eyes tensed as his right hand, forefinger pointed out, made its way towards the shiny, almost mythical looking puddle. He drew a figure eight in the red velvety liquid and then turned up his forefinger to investigate what dripped from its end. The look on his face seemed lost, yet he was captivated. His eyebrows furled, his lips tightened, and his eyes slowly closed. He began to feel dizzy and fell to his knees at the edge of the bed. He caught his upper body with his left hand on the mattress's blunt edge. He was suddenly lost in an unexpected flashback.

Steve Layton, at thirty-three, was no stranger to trauma and despair. He had been the one just three years earlier who had come home to find his wife, Debbie, in a pool of blood in their own bedroom. She was seven months pregnant at the time, with what would have been their first child. She was lying on her back on the bed. Her legs were propped up in a birthing position, with pillows stacked behind her back and neck. Between her legs was their lifeless child. Debbie was also dead.

The Coroner had ruled the birth as a miscarriage, and Debbie's death a tragic result of a massive hemorrhage. Steve had only been twenty minutes late getting home on that fateful night. He was a patrolman at the time, and after his shift had ended, he had wanted to surprise his wife by stopping to buy her some flowers and a bag of her favorite mini candy bars. He had blamed himself for their deaths ever since.

Detective Layton snapped out of his sweat-filled dreamscape. He would now have to go to Saint Stephens Hospital for the nerve racking task of interviewing the poor victim. This was the part of his job that he loathed the most, especially when the victims were women or children.

~ **4** ~

The silence of the still bedroom was broken by the telephone ring. An arm reached out from under the covers and fumbled around the night stand for a moment, in search of the receiver, "He--llo," a deep voice answered with a gruff clearing of the throat.

The voice on the other end of the line was all too familiar. "Hey baby, watcha' do'in?" a soft, but sassy voice said. It was Lindsey, a local stripper at Diamonds Adult Entertainment Club, who danced under the nickname 'Alpha'.

"Sleeping," the man's voice retorted.

"Can I come over?"

"What timc is it?"

"About 2:30. I'm just leaving work. So, do you care if I come over?" Lindsey prodded.

"If you want," the young man said just before hanging up the phone. He rolled over onto his back, sat up, rubbed his eyes and then staggered to the dimly lit bathroom to relieve himself.

About ten minutes later, a set of knuckles wrapped on the aluminum door of the apartment. A man opened the door. On the second story landing stood the invited dancer - a woman of about thirty- four years. She was dressed in knee-high white vinyl boots, a pair of Daisy Duke styled jean shorts, and a small halter top. Her wavy hair rode slightly past her shoulders and boasted a poorly kept blonde dye job, with dark brown roots. Her makeup was extremely heavy around the eyes, and the mascara was beginning to run down her weathered cheeks. Her thighs were patterned with cellulite dimples, and bulged out of her skimpy shorts, as she wore them slightly below her hipbones. A road map of light stretch marks painted her belly between her naval and the button that secured her shorts. Her nails were fake and a few of them were missing. Those remaining had chipped red nail polish on them. One of her eyebrows sported a small golden hoop. Although moderately overweight in proportion to her height of 5' 7", her breasts were nothing to cause a second glance. They were rather small considering her broad shoulders. The stretch marks on them matched her belly, and they sagged like under filled water balloons beneath the white halter. She looked as though a Mack Truck had run her over - a few times.

She entered the room and shut the door with her

heal. Crossing the small room, her jaw kept time to her steps as she rigorously smacked her gum. She flopped down on the couch like a half-filled bag of potatoes.

The young man followed her into the room. He was about 18 years old and at just 5' 8", he had a beer gut and reddish-brown hair with a balding crown. His face showed evidence of a small goatee.

He approached the couch and stood in front of Lindsey, wearing only a pair of plaid boxer shorts. He pulled the boxers down to his knees as a hint of his immediate desire. Lindsey obliged without hesitation. She took his penis into her mouth without removing her gum. She bobbed rapidly on his stiff erection for about thirty seconds before he grabbed her hair with his left hand, pulling her roughly away from his manhood. She grinned and immediately rolled over, slid her shorts off and dropped her knees to the floor. She placed her elbows on the sofa seat cushions and began to mutter, "Fuck me. Fuck me hard. Give it to me," as he slid in and out of her. He came moments later, pulled out of her, and collapsed onto the sofa next to her. He pulled a colorful blanket off the back of the couch and covered his lap.

Lindsey rose up, still smacking her gum, and half

leaped onto the couch next to him, "You were careful, weren't you?" she asked.

A look of aggravation came across his face as he slowly turned his head towards her, "Of course," he answered, "I'm always careful."

Lindsey looked over at her son and continued, "We can't afford to get caught. We have to always be careful or we'll both end up in prison... or dead."

"Ummm . . .," he said with a grumble, "I don't want to talk about that right now, mom." He leaned forward and proceeded to pull out a cigar box from underneath the couch. He set it on the Goodwill- looking coffee table in front of them and opened it. Inside were an array of small Cocaine and Meth filled baggies and other drug paraphernalia, including syringes and pipes. He poured some Meth on the table and chopped at it with a razor blade. A glint of light reflected off the blade as he slowly and calculatedly chopped it up, and made two almost symmetrical lines. Lindsey anxiously reached over to the cigar box, pulled out a sterling silver straw about three inches long and inhaled one of the lines. She then tilted her head back and shuddered. She licked her finger and ran it across the table where the Meth had been moments ago. She then licked her finger once again, tasting the bitterness as it instantly numbed her tongue. At that moment, she could think of nothing she loved more than sex and drugs.

Pray For Death

~ 5 ~

Detective Layton received a call on the police radio of his county owned, late model Ford Explorer.

The radio blared, "101... *101... come in.*"

"This is 101... Go ahead," Layton replied with a click of his mic.

"101... *Respond to a one-eight-seven at nine-eight-six Cove Road North,*" the dispatcher continued in her heavy southern drawl.

"10-4... En route."

The Detective quickly flipped the toggle switches on the dash to turn on his blue lights and siren. His foot mashed down on the gas pedal, making the engine roar under the hood.

Five minutes later he arrived at the address. It was on the west side of the county in an area called Candler. He flipped off his siren as he turned and parked on the front of a neatly manicured lawn. He had to squeeze his vehicle in between the half-dozen other public service vehicles already on the scene. They included a fire truck, an ambulance, three marked County Sheriff cars and one unmarked one. It was 6:30pm. He had been on his way home for the day when he had received the call from dispatch to respond to this scene. He knew a one-eighty-seven was a homicide, so he wasn't sure why the dispatcher had given the call to him.

He exited his vehicle and made his way across the lawn to the rather small but picturesque cottage surrounded by tall pine trees. A heavyset, female, uniformed officer met him at the front steps and directed him to follow her around to the side entrance. As he began to follow her, he looked up at the front door and noticed it was shut. There was police tape across it and two uniformed officers guarding it like a barricade. He continued to the side of the cottage. As he rounded the corner of the house and began to enter the side door into the kitchen, he glanced back to the front lawn and noticed the County Coroner's wagon entering the drive.

Layton entered through the kitchen. Inside was a scene resembling Grand Central Station. People were scurrying in every direction. Although the kitchen was well lit, Layton noticed the rest of the house was considerably dark. He began walking towards the doorway leading into the rest of the house. He slid his hands into a pair of surgical gloves just as he heard someone call out his name, "Layton, over here," the voice said.

Layton immediately saw Detective Ken Barton already standing in the foyer waving his hand, motioning for

Layton to join him.

Ken Barton was a transplant to the area from Central Florida. He was thirty-eight, about 6' tall, extremely thin, with brown hair, a brown medium-thickness mustache and a rough complexion. He had moved to the Asheville area four years earlier after a brutal divorce from his wife of nine years. She had left him for another man. He had been extremely devastated when she had taken the children and made it virtually impossible for him to see them. She had moved to Asheville while the divorce was in progress, so he had followed a few months later to be closer to his children.

Detective Layton passed through the doorway and approached Detective Barton a few steps away. They both nodded a serious businesslike greeting to each other as Layton asked, "What have we got?"

Layton hadn't noticed anything in the room yet. Detective Barton didn't speak. He just raised his right hand and pointed over Layton's shoulder towards the inside of the front door. By the look on Detective Barton's face, Layton knew he was in for a shock. He was almost afraid to turn and look, yet he knew that he had to. He felt his heart begin to beat so hard he could hear it echoing in his head. As if almost in slow motion, he turned his head and body towards the front door. He never could have imagined what he was about to see.

Hanging on the large wooden door was a woman.

"Dina Watkins," Barton said.

Layton recognized the name immediately. He knew her, not by personal acquaintance, but professional. She was a middle-aged dancer at Diamonds, whom he had busted numerous times over the last few years for things including: Drug Possession, Prostitution, DWI and Lewd & Lascivious Activity. She was hanging naked, almost 'Christ-Like', with her arms extending past the edges of the door, where they were securely fastened from wrist to elbow by three large concrete nails driven through each of them. A four inch wide leather strap crossed her body under her arms just below her rather large synthetic breasts. The strap was secured to the door at both ends with railroad ties, seemingly to support most of her weight. Her legs dangled freely below her blood covered body. Her skin was pale and her head hung down to one side, covered partly by her long, straight, blonde, blood drenched hair. Blood was still streaming slowly down her legs and dripping into a pool on the hardwood floor just inches below.

Layton felt a swell of nausea rising in his stomach. He thought for sure that he was going to hurl the entire contents of his stomach in one giant heave. He began to sweat from his brow as Detective Barton calmly said,

"Let's get this over with," as he placed a hand on Layton's shoulder. They both moved slowly toward the door to begin the scrupulous task of investigating the scene and gathering any evidence.

As they reached the body, no evident wounds were immediately visible. Layton reached up, more out of habit than anything else, to the victim's neck to feel for a pulse. As his hand approached, her head lifted up quickly and she let out a blood curdling scream.

"Geezis Fuckin' Christ!" Layton screamed, as he flew backwards and fell to the floor. He quickly scurried away on his hands and feet, still looking at her with panic-stricken horror on his face. Barton had also been caught off guard and had flown backwards into a small trinket shelf filled with mini porcelain clowns. He staggered, but did not fall as the clowns fell to the floor and shattered. He was now holding the back of his head with his left hand, checking it for any sign of his own blood. There was none.

Both Detectives looked at the woman on the door from their cowering positions. She was moving her head around frantically, as if looking to see if her attacker was still nearby. However, upon a closer look, both Detectives realized that her eye sockets were hollow. Her lips had also been cut away, exposing her teeth and gums. Blood still gurgled out of her mouth.

"Shit. Shit. What the fuck?" Barton said as he frantically paced back and forth.

Layton immediately hollered for the paramedics to come and assist, but they had already heard the scream from outside. They had raced into the house and were now putting their expertise to work. What seemed at first to be a homicide was now a frantic race to save this woman's life - no matter how pitiful it may have been.

Layton made his way through the kitchen, staggering, half attempting to lunge the distance in one leap until he reached the doorway to the outside.
There, he threw up his lunch. It hit the lower steps and the lawn below him. He pulled out his handkerchief, wiped his mouth and collapsed onto the top step. His eyes were bloodshot with tears as he clinched a fist to his chin and muttered angrily,
"I'm gonna' get this sonofabitch!"

This was the second attack and mutilation. The first, in Swannanoa, had been 3 weeks earlier.

~ **6** ~

The police station was a typical scene made up of half the public servants looking as though they were working their asses off, and the other half not really giving a shit if anyone of rank noticed they weren't. At one desk, a Detective in a short sleeved, plaid, button down shirt sat twirling a rubber band around his forefinger. Uniformed officers stood around the room gossiping about 'who's dating who', while the upper ranking officers in the room pretended not to notice.

Just then, the Sheriff walked in and the room immediately cleared, other than the seven or eight badges that should have been there to begin with.

"Barton, Layton. In my office!" the Sheriff bellowed as he made his way across the room to his glass encased office.

Detectives Barton and Layton had been sitting at their desks on the north end of the room. Detective Layton's desk backed up to a large, plate glass window on the fifth floor of the building, overlooking a beautiful downtown skyline. Barton's temporary desk faced Layton's head to head. A small Dallas Cowboys bobbing head doll sat

33

dead center on Barton's desk, surrounded by nothing out of the ordinary: A PC monitor, a stack of manila folder case files, a pencil caddy and a plain black porcelain coffee mug - every item neatly arranged. Layton's desk sported a similar decor: The Dallas bobbing head and black mug replaced by a mini Miami Dolphins helmet, and a University of Miami mug.

At the Sheriff's command, the Detectives briefly looked at each other, and then both got up and immediately headed towards his office. After a few steps, Detective Layton turned around, returned to his desk to retrieve a file folder and then attempted to catch up to Barton with a slight jog. They both entered the Sheriff's office together.
"Shut the door." the Sheriff growled.

Barton obliged as Sheriff Cagle was drawing all the blinds in the room. Both Detectives sat down without hesitation.

"So, what have we got, boys?" Cagle asked inquisitively.

Detective Barton was the first to respond.

"Well Sir," he started, almost ashamingly, "from the actual crime scenes we have absolutely nothing.

However," his voice filled with a slight exuberance, "we did get a small break after the second attack."

"Yes Sir," Layton interjected with some enthusiasm, "the actual crime scenes produced no forensic evidence, but we did run the M.O. by the F.B.I. over in Raleigh. An Agent Raney said it was similar to a series of crimes about 4 years ago… down in Titusville, Florida. The crimes were never solved, but after a year and a half, and seven slashings, the sick bastard just seemed to stop. No similar crimes have been reported over the last two years… well, at least not until now."

"Do you think this could be the same perp?" the Sheriff asked as he lit a cigarette from the pack he had been fumbling with since sitting down.

"Possibly," replied Barton, "This Agent Raney is going to come down day after tomorrow and bring us the evidence they had on those cases."

"You boys know I have a Press Conference the following day. That'll give you less than twenty-four hours to come up with something positive for me to tell the Press concerning this case," Cagle said with sweat running off his forehead, and a sense of nervousness coming across in his voice. He was now puffing frantically on his cigarette as he glanced over at one of his campaign posters on his wall. He knew the election was only a month away, and that if these crimes were still unsolved by then, it could affect the outcome of this tight campaign race. The Sheriff knew he was up against a younger, more professional, suit wearing Criminal Justice college grad, and this made him extremely nervous. He knew the outcome of this election may not be in his favor - especially if this case wasn't solved quickly.

"Well, what are you waiting for? Go catch this sonofabitch, before he cuts the whole town to shreds!" Cagle barked.
"Right"

"Yes sir"

The Detectives made a rapid departure as the Sheriff slumped down into his seat. He looked down at the pack of cigarettes still in his hand, and suddenly realized, first, that they weren't even his, and secondly, that this was the first cigarette he had lit in over five years. He quickly put out the cigarette, stood up, walked to the door of his office and nervously peered out into the station room. He crushed the pack in his left hand.

~~~~~~~~~

The Detectives made their way to the parking lot where they stopped just a few feet short of Detective Barton's unmarked, white Ford Crown Victoria. Layton turned to him and excused himself for the evening, promising to see Barton on Monday morning. It was Saturday night and Layton wanted to swing by Diamonds to ask a few questions, since most of the dancers and staff would be working. He was hoping to be able to enjoy some of the evening as well. Hell, it had been three years since Debbie had died, and he had only been laid twice since then. Both of them had been strippers from Greenville, South Carolina. He wasn't a bad looking guy that couldn't pick up a decent woman, just a little un-nervy about meeting them. He had sworn that he would never allow himself to fall in love again, and keeping a marked distance from women seemed the way to assure keeping his own promise. He also knew that most of the dancers at the club would go home with a customer for the right price. However, he was hoping to see his favorite one tonight - Charli.

~~~~~~~~~

After heading to his home on the south side of town, to shower, grab a bite to eat and restock his cigarette supply from the carton on his dresser, Layton left for the club. It was about a twenty minute drive to Leicester from his home in the middle classed housing suburb in Arden. His neighborhood was a nice development where every fourth house was the same design. Sometimes they were a different color, but overall they were almost identical, right down to the landscaping. The streets had tall lamps and concrete curbs - a rarity around this town. The homes were all three or four bedroom, two baths, some with swimming pools and others with just Jacuzzis to spoil the residents. Being in the newly developed part of town gave the real estate a higher dollar value and attracted a nice array of professional occupants. Although Layton lived alone, he enjoyed the extra room to accommodate family members who frequently stopped in unannounced from both his side of the family, as well as from Debbie's. He learned to deal with their short stays in the guest bedrooms, by spending a lot of time at work, and excusing himself to bed whenever the conversation became too boring, or jumped to the topic of Debbie's death.

As he drove up Interstate 26 towards the club, he suddenly felt as if the world was passing him in slow motion. Quick two to three second flashes were bombarding his thoughts, with visions mixed between vivid memories of making love to his wife, and the gruesome scene he had discovered that fateful night of her passing. As the flashes continued back and forth, in slow motion, the loving images of Debbie were slowly fading to visions of Charli dancing around a brass pole in the club. However, as the transformation occurred each time, for a few moments it was his pregnant wife, Debbie, on the stage - not Charli. Eventually, the bloody visions of Debbie and his child were simultaneously changing to visions of the crime scenes in this case, in alternating sequences.

Layton began to feel his blood pressure rising. The sound of his heartbeat was now pounding over the music of Joe Cocker singing *When the Night Comes*, on the CD player. This continued for what seemed like an eternity, until he suddenly snapped out of it to find himself traveling at over 100 MPH. He immediately released his foot from the accelerator of his Explorer, instantly noticing his exit had snuck up on him. He quickly veered to the circular off-ramp and noticed his headlamps reflecting off of a yellow and black sign reading 'EXIT RAMP 25 MPH'. Knowing he would never make it around the curve at his current dropping speed of 60 MPH, he jerked the steering wheel to the left, opposite the direction of the curve, in an attempt to bank the vehicle in the grass. The vehicle screeched as it swerved off the road and into the awaiting mass of green underbrush. The Explorer spun completely around twice and came to a rest in a flat clearing. Layton's arms were folded across the top of the steering wheel, with his head exhaustingly buried in them. He was almost afraid to lift his head to assess the situation. Not for fear of any physical damage or injury, but psychological.

Within a few moments, the Detective regained his composure, just about the time the CD player changed to the next song. He lifted his head, wiped the sweat from his brow and drove the vehicle slowly back to the off ramp and continued on his way.

~ 7 ~

Diamonds was far from being fancy. The building it resided in was formerly a hardware store. The conversion it had undergone, inside and out, to make it a Strip Club had been cheap, and looked as though it was completed by a Junior High shop class. It had been a fight to the bitter end when the club had applied for its Occupational License. Since Leicester was right smack in the heart of the 'Bible Belt', the physical and legal opposition had been fierce. Protestors had taken to the sidewalks almost twenty four hours a day during the remodeling period, while local churches used parishioner's donations, and held bake sales to hire their own attorneys to file suits against the county. In the end, it had all been a futile effort. The club only opened one week behind schedule, not because of any legal issues or red tape, but as a result of a back stock problem on the order placed for furniture.

Layton didn't consider himself a 'regular' to the club. Actually, he had only been there a half dozen times since it had opened. The second time was when he had met Charli. There was something intriguing about her, even though she was a stripper. He also knew she was living with someone; however, this was of little concern. Layton wasn't looking for any type of commitment, just a woman to sleep with.

Layton paid the $6 cover charge just inside the front doors and made his way, without hesitation, to the bar. He ordered a bottle of Michelob Light and propped himself up on a stool. He immediately began to pan the room with his eyes.

The room was dark, with most of its light coming from the vast array of neon beer signs that littered the walls behind the bar. A couple of young guys were playing pool on the fluorescent-lit tables in one corner of the room, while three dancers huddled in another. Their loud cackling splitting even Vince Neil's voice blaring through the enormous Peavey speakers hanging from the ceiling. He recognized the dancers, but none of them were Charli. One of them glanced up quickly and spotted him at the bar. She gave him the 'finger wave' and a sexy smile. Layton rolled his lips tight, raised his bottle and nodded his head once, more as an acknowledgement of her presence rather than a greeting. He took a swig of his beer before setting it down on the long L-shaped, varnished wooden bar. A feeling of warmth began to fill his muscles and his midsection. He loved the feeling he got when he drank beer. He never really got drunk on beer, just a really cool buzz that he could keep up almost indefinitely if he desired. He had learned years ago how to master 'the pace'. He hated getting too drunk and more so he hated throwing up. Another reason why he had given up hard liquor years earlier.

A large Budweiser clock on the wall read 9:20. It was early and Layton knew he had many hours of intoxicating fun ahead of him. He lit a Marlboro Light with his sterling silver Zippo, rose up out of his stool and strolled across the room to a wide doorway leading into another room. In this room was the action hundreds of men came to see nightly. This room was much darker than the other. The ceiling was lined with black lights and an array of discothèque and laser lights that flashed wildly about. Stretching out into the room was a large dance stage with a single brass pole in its center. Mirrors lined all the walls to give the room an enlargement effect, and a tinted glass encased DJ booth towered over the entire room. Other than the chairs surrounding the stage, the room was filled with cocktail sized tables and chairs and black leather booths along every wall. Along the far wall, raised up about four feet, was an area set aside for VIP guests. Velvet ropes blocked the access ways on either end of this area with 'VIP ONLY' written on a sign dangling from each.

Def Leppard began to blast from an array of speakers situated throughout the room. A hidden mirror-covered door suddenly swung open from the back of the stage and out came a dancer in a bright colored T-back covered by a long white see thru cape-styled dress split all the way up to her right hip. It was Charli. Layton immediately found a seat directly at the stage next to two bikers smoking excessively fat cigars. An exhilarating smile began to creep across his face. He leaned back into the leather reclining chair, rested his chin between his left hand thumb and forefinger, and stared wide-eyed at his favorite past-time. Euphoria began to set in.

Within a minute or two Charli had danced her way around the stage collecting dollar bills in her garter belt as she made her way over to where Layton anxiously awaited. He could barely remember to breathe as she dropped to her knees in front of him. Her body moved rhythmically to the background beat of *Pour Some Sugar on Me*. Through her dress he could see her nipples standing erect. Her belly button touted a glow-in-the-dark ring that matched her earrings, and the one in her brow. Her fingernails and toenails both had French manicures and glowed brightly under the black lights, as did her teeth when she smiled. Her body covered in glitter and smelling of a lilac based perfume only added to the eroticism of the moment. Layton felt his groin begin to swell as she flung herself backwards, now lying on her back in front of him, her legs spread wide, knees up, feet flat on the stage. He adjusted himself in his seat so as to position his face closer to the erotic mound that was draped only by the thin yellow material of her t-back. He could see slightly through the glowing material to make out a small thin patch of pubic hair and a long thin slit that trailed down to her ass. She began to gyrate her hips slowly, up and down in a simulated fucking motion as her fingertips lightly glided over her vagina and up and down her inner thighs, only to have this motion repeated again and again. Layton had now stopped breathing. His pants were now engorged to capacity. He was sure he was going to cum right there in his pants. Charli sat up, rolled forward, swung her legs around behind her and proceeded to lean across the mantle of the stage. She gracefully moved his beer to one side and placed both her forearms on his shoulders, hands draping over his shoulder blades. Her right cheek pressed up against his as her mild, minty breath wisped by his ear. He shuddered slightly as he felt the blood flush away from his head and face. He inhaled her scent in a long breath as her hair almost completely draped his entire head. She whispered softly in his ear, "I want you."

Layton didn't think he could handle any more without embarrassing himself, so he drew back slowly in his chair away from her magnetic grip. He tried to hide the ardor in his face but his eyes gleamed with sexual desires. He wanted to fuck her so badly he couldn't stand it. His hand shook as he reached in his front pocket, removed a stack of folded bills and slip a 5-spot in the t-strap she was seductively sliding down and outwards from her waistline. Her face changed to a pouty, almost childish stare. She glared at him for a second in appreciation, raised and lowered her eyebrows once in a quick motion, then quickly rose to her feet as the song playing ended and changed to *Love's a Bitch*.Layton began to breathe normally again as the tingle subsided from his forehead. He knew he'd have to visit the ATM machine by the front door before the night was over.

~~~~~~~~~

The dressing room at Diamonds was always a world of its own. Being the most well lit room in the entire building made it far from a sexy scene. Although completely naked and half-naked women were ever-present, the positions and acts being performed would probably only be desirable to Marilyn Manson. From the insertions of tampons, nose hair plucking, gargling and spitting, gum smacking and toilets flushing, to earwax swabbing and the grotesque and intentional lifting of legs to pass gas, followed by a round of giggles. It was definitely not the erotic scene embedded in a teenager's wet dream.

On any given night there were between five and fifteen dancers setting up their temporary privy in the
~~~~~~~~~

dressing room. Tonight being Saturday, capacity was at its max. These were women from all walks of life, each with their own depressing story of why they do what they now do. Some claiming to be forced into it by the hardships of life, while others claimed the lure of quick and easy cash would propel them from this temporary occupation into something better for themselves and in most cases for their children.

An overweight cocktail waitress dressed in a black leotard, fishnet stocking and 4" heels replaced Layton's bottle with a fresh one. He paid the $3.75 and left her the change from the $5 bill. After finishing his beer and ordering another, he had almost completely forgotten that he had also come to the club to inquire about the two dancers who had their faces amateurly reconstructed. He lit another cigarette as he rose to reposition himself on a couch along the back wall. A few minutes later, after completing her set on stage, Charli joined him. Not so gracefully though, as she strolled across the room in her 6" white heels. She awkwardly plopped herself down beside him on the low rise couch, almost sitting on top of him. Layton didn't mind. He just shifted over quickly to make room for her beautiful ass coming towards him. She spilled a little of his beer on his crotch and instinctively grabbed his beverage napkin from the palm of his hand, and obligingly patted the wet spot on his pants, looking up at his face every couple of seconds, almost as if searching for a look of approval. She got it through an awry grin.

"So, how have you been?" he began.
"Okay and you?"

"Pretty good, considering." Layton replied.

"Considering what?" she asked as the scent of sour-apple vodka radiated from her tonsils, as she delicately balanced a martini glass on her knee.

He decided not to answer the question directly. Instead, he asked, "Where's your friend Dina, tonight?" He prodded in a deceitfully innocent manner, knowing good and well exactly where she was.

An initial look of shock came across her face, subtlety replacing her sensual smile, "She's in the hospital, Steve. She was attacked earlier today by some psychopath who ripped her face apart."

He pretended to gasp a little and act surprised.

She continued, "I don't know the exact details, but it was the talk of the dressing room this evening. I'm going to go and see her at the hospital tomorrow." Her eyes began to fill with tears.

"God, I'm really sorry Charli," he said with bona-fide compassion. He *did* have compassion for Dina. Who couldn't have?

"I hear she had her arms cut off and her eyes gouged out," she continued as a lump came to her throat.

Layton knew that this was only partially true, but he didn't want her to know that he knew this privileged information.

"Wow," he expressed solemnly, "who the hell would want to do that to her?"

"Who fucking knows? I can't imagine anyone doing something so horrific. I wish I did know," a sense of anger replaced her sorrow, "I'd kill the sonofabitch! It was probably some sick fuckin' bastard customer from in here!" She nervously glanced around the room, "That's what scares the piss out of me. She's the second girl from the club to be attacked in a month. Did you hear about the first?"

Steve continued to play the innocence charade, "Yeah, I think I did read something in the paper about another attack. You think it was the same person?"

"I don't want to even think about it," she said matter-of-factly, trying to end the topic.

Layton knew not to pry any further. He motioned in the air for the cocktail waitress to come over. He lit a cigarette and handed it to Charli, then followed up with one for himself. The waitress bounced over in her giddy manner. Layton told her to get Charli whatever she wanted to drink and another beer for himself. She smiled and trotted off.

Steve and Charli just sat there silently for a few minutes puffing on their cigarettes and eyeballing the girl who had now taken the stage. She was a pretty girl, about 18 or 19 years old. She had vine ripe, solid, perky breasts, a small waist and one tattoo on each extremity. They were nothing forbidding or deviant: A butterfly, a teddy bear, a rose and someone's name. Charli stared intently at her, and with good reason. She was one of her lovers.

The waitress returned and delivered their drinks. Layton paid for them and reclined comfortably back into the leather that surrounded him. Charli instinctively snuggled up close to him as she sipped on her Angel's Breast Martini. For the moment, they were both comfortable just relishing the warmth between them. Charli felt secure with him, unlike most of her customers. She almost wished she had met him under different circumstances.

~ 8 ~

Deputy Willy Biddle had picked up a graveyard patrol on Saturday night for a sick coworker. He actually preferred this shift over the A.M. shift, but had been unable to secure a permanent spot on the shift due to his short time on the force. Tonight he was assigned to the west side of town consisting of Patton Avenue, New Leicester Highway and parts of Enka-Candler. It was 10:00pm and Patton Avenue was beginning to jump with activity. The usual long trail of cruising cars were beginning their half-mile loop down the street to Leicester Highway-- only to turn around, cruise slowly back down Patton Avenue, to Denny's restaurant, and u-turn again. This cycle would continue for the next two to three hours. The vast majority of these 'cruisers' were male teenagers on the prowl, keeping high, but misguided hopes that they might actually pick up someone of the opposite sex.

Willy's main responsibility tonight would be to watch over this amateur parade, in the effort to keep traffic flowing smoothly and to keep the peace. Although considered a shitty patrol by most of the other deputies, Willy actually liked it. He liked knowing that he had a specific task, as opposed to the usual shift consisting of just riding around until something happened.

He slowly maneuvered his patrol car in and out of the lanes of traffic, feeling almost as if he was back in his own Datsun B210, cruising this very strip just a few years earlier.

Willy had grown up in Asheville, in the Hill Street Projects. Having ridden the 'short buses his entire life, he had never realized what a disadvantaged life he had lived. He had always been a happy-go-lucky kid with an ever plastered smile on his face -- or as the other kids called it, a 'perma-grin'. Because he was also extremely skinny and awkward, and not functioning with a full deck, he was teased all the time. However, it never bothered Willy. Mostly because he mistook all the taunting and attention to mean that the neighborhood kids liked him and always wanted to play with him. Of course it probably was also fueled by his mother telling him things like, "They aren't making fun of your thick glasses, Willy. They are just jealous that they don't have any."

Willy wasn't technically classified as retarded, so he was still eligible for inclusion on the Police Force. He had passed the preliminary police exam by only one point over the minimum required score.

The 'Thump-Thump' of audio bass could be felt and

heard for blocks. The familiar scent of vendors' boiled peanuts filled the cool night air. Willy decided to pull into the old Firestone parking lot to get a bag. From the elevated lot he would be able to eat them and still have a grandstand view of the traffic below. He turned his cruiser onto Louisiana Avenue and immediately rolled into the oversized parking lot that connected a multitude of businesses. There were no other vehicles in the lot other than the white dually truck towing a carnival-style food trailer.

Willy parked at the edge of the paved lot, overlooking the street below. He exited his vehicle and walked over to the trailer. He purchased a small bag of boiled peanuts and strolled back to his car. He leaned inside the driver's window and turned up his police radio, then perched himself on his hood.

~~~~~~~~

Meanwhile, only about a mile away, Detective Layton was far from sober now. Although his demeanor was calm and collective, he was having difficulty focusing on any one spot in the room. There was a slight blur to his vision and his eyes jumped around the room in a quick, jerky motion. Charli had gone to the dressing
~~~~~~~~

room to pee and freshen up her makeup -- something she did frequently throughout each evening.

A man sat down on the sofa next to Layton. The Detective rolled his head around to see who it was, but was unable to focus enough to see his face clearly. Through the blur, he could only tell that the man wasn't very large and sported a goatee. The man was silent, just sitting there nonchalantly, staring straight forward like a stunned lizard. Another dancer had taken the stage as Neil McCoy 'boot- scooted' off the mirrored walls. A few moments later, not having said a word, the man rose up off the couch and disappeared into the now fairly large crowd. A moment later Charli returned.

As Layton wobbly looked up at her, she noticed a small, white, ring-sized box sitting on the sofa cushion next to him. She picked up the box and pivoted almost mechanically on one heel and dropped her derrière to the awaiting cushion next to him. As she pondered over the box, an elicit smile crept across her face. 'Had *he bought her a ring? A charm? Earrings? How sweet!'* she thought.

"Is this for me?" she asked excitedly.

Layton replied with a dumbfounded look on his face, "What?"

"Oh don't play games, Steve. Can I open it?" she

said as she began to lift the lid.   "Huh, What--" He was interrupted by a deafening scream.

Charli dropped the box between them and jumped to her feet, shaking her hands next to her face in disgust. Her screams now faded to whimpering squeals, her face overcome with a morbid glare.

Layton had felt the box hit his right leg when it had dropped. He had hesitated for a moment as Charli had gone airborne, but now reached down to see what was next to his thigh. He felt around in the dim light, not having a clue what to expect. His hand finally came across something and his dead facial expression changed to a bewildered one in an instant. He grabbed the item between his pointer finger and his thumb and raised it up towards his face to get a better look. He blinked hard as he forced his eyes to focus on the item. His vision cleared slowly. In his grip was a human eyeball.

~~~~~~~~~

Deputy Biddle heard his radio crackle once, then the dispatcher's voice, "All *units in the vicinity of New Leicester Highway and Patton Avenue...Respond to a ten-sixty-seven   at   Diamonds   Nightclub...Diamonds*
~~~~~~~~~

Nightclub."

Willy immediately slid off the hood and reached inside the window of his cruiser. Another voice had already come across the radio, "This *is 1-11 responding...ETA four minutes."*

Willy climbed inside the car and queued up his mic, "This is 1-0-9... En route." He already had his cruiser in reverse and was smoking up his tires. He slammed the gear shift down hard into DRIVE, almost skipping NEUTRAL altogether. He flipped on his lights and siren.

"1-0-9... *1-0-9"* the dispatcher said emotionless

"This is 1-0-9... Go ahead."

"1-0-9... *What's your ETA?"*

"Less dan' a minute" Willy responded.

"Stand *fast 1-0-9... Stand fast and await further instructions."*

"Roger dispatch...Standing fast at the corner of Leicester and Patton," Willy said obediently as he rounded the corner onto Leicester Highway. He quickly checked his rear-view mirror. When he saw that no one was behind him, he halted his vehicle and then crossed the oncoming traffic to enter the parking lot of the Sisters of Mary Health Clinic. He rolled his cruiser around and positioned it facing the street and placed it in PARK. He shut off his siren, but left his overhead blues on. He grabbed a soggy peanut from the bag on the passenger seat and awaited further instruction.

~~~~~~~~~~

The music was now off and the house lights had been brought up, lighting the entire club. All the customers had been herded to the pool table room by the management and bouncers. Surprisingly enough, Detective Layton had kept his cool when he found himself staring into a solitary green iris. He had pulled out his handkerchief and gently placed the ping pong ball sized organ into it, and had placed it gently on the black sofa. He had then stepped up to the DJ booth, held his badge up and ordered the long haired jockey to shut off the music and raise the lights. The jockey hadn't even hesitated to oblige.

The look on most of the customers' faces was of confusion and curiosity. Most had no clue what was going on, but none were happy about having to stick around to be questioned by the police.

Layton had taken control of the scene, as best he
~~~~~~~~~~

could, considering his inebriated state of mind. Surprisingly though, the incident had jolted him into a clearer state of mind, along with the extra strong coffee he was now drinking.

Just moments after the lights came up, a couple of dancers had seen a young man run out the emergency exit in the rear hall. One dancer had been too stoned to care, while the other had thought enough to watch what kind of vehicle he got into. It was a red, full-sized, extended cab pickup truck. She had told Detective Layton that she believed it to be a Chevy or GMC. Using his cell phone, Layton had already been on the line with a central dispatch officer. He had relayed this info to her, and she had immediately dispatched it over the radio.

Deputy Biddle now had a description of the vehicle, and within a minute or two, had spotted the truck heading southbound on Leicester Highway, crossing directly in front of him at a high rate of speed.
Willy immediately pulled out onto the roadway and took chase. He radioed into dispatch, "Central...this is 1-0-9." He waited for a response.

"Central...*Go ahead 1-0-9.*"

"This is Willy–," he corrected himself, "This is 1-0-9...

I'm in pursuit of da' red suspect truck," his voice filled with excitement, "heading weth'bound on Patton."

Willy's patrol car was sliding sideways as he rounded the curve, smoke billowing from his spinning tires. He had a look of determination on his face, with a small smile creeping to his lips every few moments. This was his first high speed chase. He felt and electrifying sense throughout his body as he feathered the gas pedal around the winding curves. A single drop of sweat now beaded down his right cheek. For a fleeting moment he almost forgot that he was a police officer in a high speed pursuit of a wreck less, fleeing suspect. 'Suspect *of what?*' Willy wondered. He felt for a moment, as though he were Jeff Gordon, his favorite NASCAR driver, in a relentless pursuit of the #9 car in front of him.

"All *available units, assist 1-0-9,*" The message from the dispatcher repeated, "All *available units assist 1-0-9*".

The chase continued erratically westbound on Patton Avenue, which eventually became Smokey Park Highway. Two other Sheriffs and a State Trooper now joined in the chase from behind Deputy Biddle. The red truck was driving as if the person behind the wheel had no regard for his own safety -- climbing onto curbs, weaving in and out of heavy traffic, clipping and sideswiping numerous cars and trucks as it traveled at speeds well over 60 MPH down the winding road.

Deputy Biddle kept a short but safe distance back from the truck, to avoid the debris that was flying through the air with each contact the truck made with other vehicles. A few moments later, the truck swerved right, into a Wendy's parking lot and locked up its brakes, leaving two black tire trails and a cloud of smoke behind it. Instantly, the heavily tinted rear slide window opened and the muzzle of an AR-15 assault rifle emerged.

Willy's cruiser had come to a screeching halt almost on the truck's rear bumper. Willy had begun to open his door when he noticed the rifle. He instinctively ducked below the dashboard onto the seat, as a spray of bullets entered the top of his windshield. Willy struggled to free his department issued 9mm pistol from the holster on his right side. It finally came loose. He was trying not to panic. He was taking deep breaths, in through his nose and out through his mouth. Sweat was now streaming down his face. He had surely not expected anything like this to happen. He knew he was too close to the truck to be safe. He knew he had to back his car up to a safer range. He could hear the screams of bystanders as another fleet of military grade, 7.62mm rounds pierced the lower half of his windshield, under the first set of shattered holes. They penetrated through the headrest of the cruiser's vinyl seat, sending yellowish colored foam stuffing flying in every direction. Willy counted to three in a whisper, using his fingers on his left hand. He then quickly sat up in the driver's seat, slammed the car into REVERSE, and rammed his foot down on the accelerator. He didn't even look back. His eyes were focused on the business end of the black rifle that still pointed in his direction.

His cruiser only traveled back about ten feet, before it slammed into another police car and stopped abruptly. Willy looked over his shoulder with a surprised look on his face, and then turned back towards the truck in front of him. He instantly heard a 'crack' and a 'whizzzz', as a single bullet ripped into his throat, and exited through the back of his neck. His head flew back against the headrest and then bounced forward, causing his body to follow. His forehead came to rest on the top of the steering wheel, as blood gushed out of his mouth and nose. His body twitched and convulsed, as he lay forward, eyes wide open in a blank stare. He blinked once. A second later, another bullet ripped into his forehead, simultaneously sending pieces of skull and brain matter exploding out the back of his head. His body flew back against the seat, and then slumped down slowly over the center console area.

The truck then jumped the curb that separated the Wendy's parking lot from the next one, and sped through the adjoining lot, racing off down a side street. Two Sheriffs immediately began to run up to Willy's patrol car but slowed down as soon as they noticed the spray of blood on the shattered rear window. They knew there was nothing they could do to save him.

~ **9** ~

At 11:15pm, Stan Seagle, the Chief Medical Examiner and Forensics Investigator, arrived at the chaotic scene at Diamonds. A dozen police cars, including Sheriffs, State Police, County Detectives, and D.O.T. filled the parking lot and overflowed onto the sidewalk. Two heavyset D.O.T. officers were strolling back from the 24 hour convenience store next door with 3 dozen doughnuts in their arms. A large bouncer with a rebel bandana covering his shaved head stood at the front door talking with two Sheriffs. Customers were now filing over the grass and curbs in their vehicles and making their way to destinations unknown.

Seagle, 46, was a tall, muscular man, almost 6'5". He had a clean shaved head accented by a thick brown Tom Selleck styled mustache and bushy eyebrows. He carried himself with an air of confidence, yet barely ever smiled. When working, he kept his eyebrows furled, causing the skin between them to wrinkle -- a look of intense concern. He had a gruff, but stern voice that commanded respect. It probably matured to that from the 20 years he had spent as a doctor in the Navy.

He entered the club through the front door. He asked the trashy leather faced man in the mismatched suit, whom he assumed to be the club's manager, where Detective Layton was. The man pointed at the stage through the inside doorway. Seagle made his way over to him, an orange box resembling a fishing tackle box, in his left hand.

"Stan."

"Steve."

The two men greeted each other with a firm handshake.

"How's the wife?" Layton asked.

"Still as anorexic as ever. Nothing new."

"Sorry to hear that."

"Thanks. What have you got?" Seagle said, quickly changing the subject to business at hand.

Layton lifted the handkerchief from the stage behind him and slowly unwrapped it, "An eyeball...human," he stated just as he exposed it.

"Hmmm," Seagle reached out, carefully took the handkerchief and eyeball from the Detective and studied it thoroughly through his spectacles, "any idea who it belongs to?"

"Yup."

Seagle peered up, without moving his head, with a slightly surprised look on his face, "Really? Who?"

Layton looked around the room to make sure no one was within earshot. He hesitated momentarily as a uniformed officer walked by. He quickly glanced around again, and then stated, "It probably belongs to a dancer that worked here."

"I'm listening."

"I'd bet the farm on it."

Seagle didn't seem amused by Layton's choice of words.

Layton felt a bit stupid for a brief moment, but continued, "Her name is Dina. Earlier this evening we found her nailed to the inside of her front door with her eyes gouged out."

"So obviously the eyes had been taken from that victim?"

"Yes, and her lips."

"Her lips?"

"Yeah. The psycho also used a razor blade or a scalpel to slice her lips off." Layton explained.

"Same suspect as that other attack a few weeks ago?" Seagle asked.

"Possibly...no fingerprints at either scene, so nothing to compare except an extremely sharp instrument was used to cut both victims up."

"I wonder why he leaves them alive. Probably a ritual of some kind." Seagle inquired.

"I don't think so. I think it's much deeper than that. I think it's a personal hatred towards these individuals, women in general, or maybe even just strippers."

Seagle folded the handkerchief back over the eyeball, "Can I borrow this?" he said – referring to the handkerchief. "Keep it."

The Medical Examiner received a text message as he was exiting the nightclub. He stopped briefly to read the message, '**Officerkilled - - Wendy's Restaurant - - Smokey Park Hwy - - 15 minutes ago.**'

Seagle showed no emotion as he clipped the pager back on to his belt, got into the car and drove off to the next crime scene at the Wendy's restaurant.

A cheesy rendition of 'Turkey in the Straw' began playing out loud, and a few different officers, including Detective Layton, all checked their cell phones. Layton answered his and listened as a voice on the other end informed him that Deputy Biddle had been shot and killed by the suspect that fled the nightclub.

"Did they get the sonofabitch?" he exclaimed.
"No?... Goddamnit!... Well, who's on it?" He asked. "Barton...Okay, I'll call the Sheriff...I'm on my way to the scene." He hung up his phone. "Shit," he whispered as he shook his head back and forth.

A phone rang in the darkness. A woman's arm reached up from the bed and switched on the lamp on the night stand. She picked up the phone, "Hello?" Betty Joe said in a tired, groggy voice. "Just a moment Steve, I'll wake him."

She glanced at the digital clock next to the phone. It read 11:48 PM. She then rolled over and shook her husband, "James," she said softly. "James, wake up

James."

The Sheriff snorted and cleared his throat, "Yeah, what? What is it?"

"James, it's Steve Layton, and he says it's urgent. Take the phone." She stretched the cord across her body and waved it over him. The Sheriff growled from the back of his throat as he sat up and took the receiver from his wife.

"This better be good!" he scoffed into the phone.

"Sheriff, I've got some bad news." Layton paused as he drummed up the strength to break the bad news, "Deputy Biddle is dead, sir," Layton informed him.

"Geezis!" The Sheriff quickly propped himself up in his bed, "How?"

"He was shot sir."

A lump formed in the Sheriff's throat. In a low solemn voice he asked his wife, "Betty, can you put on some coffee?"

"Of course dear," she replied.

A distraught feeling came over the Sheriff. He had

feared this day might come. He had had mixed feelings about Willie joining the force. He had known Willie since he was 6 years old. He had coached his little league baseball team for three different years and had spent a lot of time with him when he volunteered at the YMCA. Since joining the force, the Sheriff had tried to take Willie under his wing and keep him close to him by putting him on the day shift, but he knew Willie was a 'wild spirit' and longed for more adventure. This was not the first time Willie had picked up a night shift.

"When did it happen, Steve?"

"Less than an hour ago, sir. The M.E. is on the scene, along with Detective Barton. I'm on my way over there now. I think you should join us sir, there's something else I need to tell you about."

"Where at?"

"Wendy's." His voice lowered to a solemn tone, "How ironic, huh, Sheriff?"

"Yeah," the Sheriff said admittedly. He also knew that Willy's wife's name was Wendy. They had only been married a year.

"On the west side?" Cagle asked.

"Yes sir."

"I'll be there in 30 minutes."

The Sheriff hung up the phone and got out of bed. Betty Joe brought him a cup of coffee as he was getting dressed. He took a sip then set the cup on the night stand by his side of the bed. Betty Joe immediately picked up the mug, sat a folded napkin down and replaced the mug on top of it, not saying a word.

Betty Joe had been taking care of Buster for nearly three decades. A task she never minded. She also never asked Buster about work, and he rarely volunteered any information. But she knew by the deep, sorrowful look on his face, and the tears welling up in his eyes, that something was terribly wrong - something personal.

"Honey," she said softly and cautiously, "what is it?" She softly placed a hand on his shoulder.

Busters' hands were trembling as he attempted to slide his belt through the loops on his pants. He looked up from his now seemingly impossible task, and into Betty Joe's eyes. They were always so warm and compassionate. She stood there, distinguished in her pearl colored silk nightgown as she awaited his answer.

Although approaching fifty, she had weathered well through the years and looked all of ten years her junior. She had shoulder length golden blonde hair, ravishing blue eyes with thick dark eyelashes, and a smooth complexion to go with her perfectly straight teeth. She was always soft spoken and rarely ever raised her voice. She had studied theology in college and had the perfectly divine ability to find the good in everything and everyone.

Buster slowly raised his right hand to her left cheek and rubbed it softly with his thumb. "Willy Biddle was killed tonight, Baby." Silence followed as Betty Joe's face became expressionless. Her eyes sank as the impact of what her husband said sank in. She slowly sat down on the edge of the bed. Buster followed and put his arms around her. She began to sob as if she had lost one of her own children. Buster held her tight.

~~~~~~~~~

Buster arrived at Wendy's restaurant just as the M.E.'s vehicle pulled out of the lot. A grim look replaced his designated stare. The press had already surrounded the area, held back by sawhorse barricades covered by yellow police tape. A local television reporter yelled "Sheriff, do you have any idea who did this?" As Buster made his way to the battered police cruiser ignoring the
~~~~~~~~~

reporter.

"Where the hell is Layton?" Buster bellowed out to an officer standing nearby.

"There, sir." the officer replied pointing towards the Detective emerging from the convenience store next door.

Layton walked up to the Sheriff and fumbled with a bottle of Pepto Bismol, shifting it from his right hand to his left. He took a big swig, swallowed and then shook the Sheriff's hand.

"What the hell's wrong with you boy?" Buster grumbled.

"Nothing, sir. Just a queasy stomach."

"Oh, that's understandable." Cagle glanced over at the bullet riddled police car.

Layton had been referring to his excessive intake of booze earlier, but decided not to mention the miscommunication.

"You can fill me in later on what happened here. You mentioned you had something else to tell me. What is it?"

"Well sir, I was over at Diamonds earlier"

"Diamonds?" the Sheriff interrupted with a look of surprise. Then disapproval.

"Yes Diamonds. I'll explain why later."

"Humph." The Sheriff folded his arms.

"Anyhow, someone left an eyeball next to me on the couch."

"An eyeball?"

"Yes sir. I believe it's from the dancer we had found nailed to the door."

"On a couch?"

"Oh, yes sir. Ummm, well, you see, I was at the club trying to gather some information-"

"Whatever, Steve." The Sheriff interrupted as he held up his hand to signal he didn't even care to hear the bullshit and that silence would be in the Detective's best interest.

Layton looked down at the ground and shuffled his feet around.

"So this eyeball--" the Sheriff continued inquisitively.

"Yes sir?"

"--You called Seagle?"

"Right away. He picked it up just before he came over here."

"Did you see who left it there?"

"Well, no sir." Layton answered ashamingly.

"No?" The Sheriff seemed slightly puzzled.

"No." Layton answered again.

The Sheriff raised his eyeballs inquisitively but almost afraid to continue the conversation. "So you have no idea who left you this eyeball to find?"

"No sir." Layton lowered his head.

"Well whoever left it knew who you were."

Layton's eyes lit up enlightened. "I guess your right sir. But who?"

The Sheriff's tone immediately turned angry,

"Find out Steve! Goddamnit Boy, you find out! You find this sick fucking bastard! You get the Mother Fucker and you get him good, you hear?"

"Yes sir, I will."

"It'll be your ass if you don't Layton." the Sheriff threatened as he retreated to his car.

Layton took a huge gulp of Pepto, wiped his mouth, and took a last glance at the scene before leaving.

~~~~~~~~

The Detective drove up onto the Blue Ridge Parkway and set his speed at 35. He needed some time to think and the parkway always offered up a tranquil environment to do so. As usual for this time of night the road was quiet and traffic virtually nonexistent. The Detective drove for over an hour constantly reviewing everything he knew in his head. His frustration about the lack of evidence was giving him a headache. He took a Goody powder from his center console and unwrapped the wax paper. As he held it steady trying not to spill any white powder on the upholstery and he suddenly had a whim. He stared at the white powder in his hand. 'Cocaine?' Yes he thought 'It *resembles cocaine! Could this be the connection? A clue? The motive?*' Layton
~~~~~~~~

knew he had to talk to the girls at the club, but his cover was now blown. He would have to do it officially or would he? He knew it was time to turn up the heat. It was time to call Marcus. Layton turned his vehicle around and drove for home.

~ 10 ~

The cue ball slammed into the eight ball and sent it ricocheting off the sidewall and into the corner pocket. A massive forearm extended to shake the opponents hand. As the two locked carpals a $20 bill slipped into Marcus' other hand.

"Good game dude"

"You to," Marcus said with his usual jubilant smile.

The air in the small tavern was stale and thick with smoke. The jukebox was playing *Love Me When I'm Gone*, by 3 Doors Down, in the background, while the ethnically diverse crowd of about 15, drank mostly Pabst Blue Ribbon and talked mostly of environmental issues. The bartender sported an array of medieval style tattoos emerging from his Nike tank top. A single cocktail waitress was smoking a clove cigarette while perched at the corner of the small black Formica bar.

Marcus was definitely a familiar face in here. As a matter of f act, he was quite familiar in many places just like this around the county. Among other things, it's how he mostly supported himself - And he seemed to be doing quite well.

Marcus was an incredibly intelligent individual with a knack for style. He had a 'suave' demeanor with the ladies, while able to interact fittingly with most any crowd making his friends many and his enemies few. Although a street hustler of porn & adult toys, he made most of his money with a pool stick. Knowing almost half the nightlife people in Asheville also made him well connected in the information department. Not much happened around town without Marcus knowing about it. He was no snitch though.

It was 11:45pm on Sunday night. The bartender hollered "Last call for alcohol!", as he wiped down the bar with a dirty rag. A few customers immediately made their way to the bar to order a last round. Marcus didn't drink, but loved to engage in the Nightlife Scene. Being built like a 'Brick Shit House' didn't come from smoking either. Although it bothered him to be surrounded by it all night, he endured it as a 'hazard of the job'.

As Marcus said his 'farewells' to most of the patrons, his cell phone rang. He looked at the Caller ID, but didn't recognize the number.

"Hello?" He answered.

"Hey Marcus"

"Yeah?" he said, still unsure of the caller's identity.

"I need your help" the voice on the other end said.

"Who is this?"

"Someone who can help you to see your daughter again"

"Who the fuck is this!"

"A friend Meet me in twenty minutes at Club Illusions downtown"

"Tell me who the hell you are first!"

"A friend twenty minutes Club Illusions"

"How will I know who you are?" --- The line went dead

Marcus seemed a bit disturbed and confused by the call, but curiosity and intrigue were overwhelming his thought process. He knew he had to meet this stranger. If for no other reason than to find out what he knew about his daughter. He got into his 2000', sporty, black, 2-door Mazda RX-8 and headed for downtown. His eyebrows furled as he struggled to figure out who this mysterious stranger might be. An old friend, an acquaintance of his ex-wife, a cop? No one came to mind.

He arrived at the club five minutes early and went in. As usual, the employees and many of the customers recognized him and greeted him exuberantly. However, Marcus didn't seem his usual, smiling self. He acknowledged all of them, yet kept a determined look on his face, as he monitored the large crowd for someone that could be the caller.

He made his way through the congested crowd to a bar in the rear. He ordered a bottled water from the cute, petite barmaid and slowly sipped on it while continuing to pan over the crowd. The Techno music was excessively loud and the dance floor was full of sweaty, gyrating bodies. Discothèque lights flashed about wildly as the DJ overdid the dry ice smoke filling the club. A moment later, a hand came from behind him and rested on his right shoulder. Marcus turned to see who it was. He immediately recognized Detective Layton and rolled his eyes.

"Shit I should have known it was you," Marcus said disgustingly.

"Keepin' your nose clean, Marcus?"

"Of course."

Marcus took a sip of his water and placed the bottle on the bar.

"What the hell do you want, Layton?" Marcus asked, trying not to have anyone notice he was speaking to the Detective.

"I need your help on something, and I think I can help you in return," Layton replied.

"Help me? I'm not in any trouble!" Marcus said defensively.

"Maybe not, but when was the last time you saw your daughter?"

"That's none of your fucking concern!" Marcus said in an irritated tone.

"No, it probably isn't, but I'm sure it's been one of yours."

"And how would you be able to help me see my daughter?"

"I have a couple of buddies down at DSS. You know I can make some phone calls that could change your whole situation. I know you were railroaded by your ex, and DSS ended up fucking you over on your visitation."

"You're goddamn right they fucked me over!" Marcus exclaimed loudly, and then quickly lowered his voice again, so as not to clue anyone around to his conversation. He looked around him to see if anyone was eavesdropping. No one appeared to be, but Marcus was uncomfortable talking to the Detective in such a public place. He suggested they leave the club and meet at the abandoned Highlands Furniture warehouse on Haywood Road in fifteen minutes. It seemed, to Marcus, to be a secure place, as it had a parking lot in the rear, was dark and surrounded by tall trees. Marcus's biggest concern was still to make sure that no one would see him speaking to the Detective. This could jeopardize his reputation.

Layton agreed to meet him there and then left first. Marcus finished his bottled water in one large gulp, said goodbye to the bartender and left a few minutes later.

Layton parked in the rear lot of the warehouse, close to the building. He got out of his vehicle and quickly surveyed the dark lot, then entered the building through a rickety door hanging only by its lower hinge.

Inside, the warehouse was dark and dusty. Cobwebs stretched between the interior columns and held fast in every corner. Other than the remnants of the presence of drug users hanging out to smoke crack and shoot up, the large one-roomed warehouse was empty. Layton made a quick circle around the room as broken glass crunched under his feet. By the time he made it back to the rear door, a set of headlights rolled around the parking lot as Marcus arrived. Marcus quickly exited his car and briskly made his way inside. He spotted the Detective lighting a cigarette near a support pillar a few feet away and approached him.

"Let's be quick about this," Marcus said nervously.

"Sure." Layton held out his pack of cigarettes to offer Marcus one.

"You know I don't smoke," Marcus said irratatedly, "Those things will kill you."

Layton withdrew the pack and placed them in his coat pocket, "They'll have to get in line then," Layton replied jokingly.

Marcus was hardly amused and replied, "What do

you need Detective?"

"Right, right. Well, I'm sure you've heard, on the news, about the recent mutilations haven't you?"

"I don't watch the news but, yes, I heard about them."

"Did you know either victim?" Layton asked.

"Yeah...both."

Layton looked surprised at first, but then remembered who he was speaking with.

"I need some help with this one, Marcus."

"Help? How the fuck can I help you? I don't know who did it!"

"Maybe you don't but I still think you can help me find out who did."

"How?"

"Because you have connections."

"Connections?" Marcus said, as if he hadn't a clue what the Detective was referring to.

"Don't play dumb with me, Marcus. You know every drug dealer, pimp, two-bit hooker and stripper within a hundred miles of here and maybe more."

Marcus couldn't help but to smirk a little. To him, this was really a compliment, "So?"

"What do you mean, *so?* You know both the women were strippers. That means that they ran in your circles."

"And?"

"And... And, I think the guy who did this, probably knew the dancers and--"

Marcus interrupted abruptly, "Wait just a fucking minute, man! You're not accusing me, are you?" Marcus defensively retorted.

"Geezis Christ, Marcus! No...Do I have to spell it out for you though?"

"Oh...You think I might know who did it."

"Bada Bing! Someone give this man a prize!" Layton said in a sarcastic game show host's voice.

"Fuck you!"

"Look Marcus, I just think that drugs may have played a role in all of this. Both girls had traces of Meth in their systems. It's a long shot, but maybe their supplier is a link."

"A link?"

"Yeah, he may even be the one who did it."

"I doubt that, man."

"Huh?" Layton seemed baffled by Marcus's surety.

"Ain't no dealer gonna' slice up his best customers."

"Why not?"

"Hello... That would be stupid!"

"Why?" Layton seemed confused.

"Do I have to spell it out *for you?*" Marcus loved having the chance to demean the Detective, as he had done to him moments ago. "Strippers are top customers to them in this town. Dealers make a fortune just off of them alone. Plus, the girls are the dealer's connection to a lot more business."

"How's that?"

"Are you sure you're a Detective, man? Come on. The dancers supply their customers with all the drugs they need. And where do you think they get the stuff from?"

"Oh, right." Layton tried to act as if he knew this all along, but had just had a brain freeze. "Ok, but what if the girls owed a dealer a lot of money or something? Couldn't that piss off the dealer and have him do something violent?"

"Man you've been watching too many movies!"
Layton had thought he might have been on the right track until a few moments of conversation with Marcus. Now, he felt like he was back to square one.

"Look man, no dealer did this," Marcus reiterated.

"You're sure?"

"What did I just say? Yeah, trust me on this one."

Layton fired up another cigarette and shuffled his feet a bit on the broken glass beneath them.

Marcus looked at his watch, "Is that all?"

"Actually, no. I still need your help."

"Come on man," Marcus said exhaustingly.

"Seriously I need you to frequent the strip club."

"Man, I don't hang out there."

"Well, now you do."

"Why the fuck do you want me to do that?"

"I need you to be my eyes and ears in there," Layton explained.

"Hell no! HE-E-E-LL NO! I ain't a fucking snitch."

"I'm not asking you to snitch."

"Then what are you askin'?"

"I just want you to watch who might be acting weird or obsessive around the girls, and let me know," Layton tried to clarify.

"That's fucking snitching!"

"Marcus, I don't give a shit right now about anything illegal that's going on in there, except trying to catch this bastard. You know those girls. Don't you want this sick sonofabitch caught?"

"Yeah."

"So, how about helping me then?"

"And what guarantee can you give me about my daughter?"

"No guarantees, but I'll do the best I can."

Marcus thought the Detective was mostly full of shit about helping him with his daughter and he let him know with his facial expression. However, his daughter meant the world to him and he couldn't let an opportunity like this pass him by...If it was for real.

"Alright, man. I'll do it," Marcus finally said reluctantly.

"Good." Layton put his hand out to shake Marcus's, but he just turned and headed for the doorway.

"I'll contact you in a few days," Layton yelled after him.

Marcus didn't acknowledge.

Pray For Death

~ 11 ~

Six o'clock Monday morning came quickly. Layton had barely slept in the last few days. He shut off his alarm clock, groaned and threw his legs over the side of the bed. He held his head in his hands for a moment, and then glanced out the window at the frigid rain.

"Shit. Just what I fucking need."

He rose up slowly, cracked his neck from side to side and made his way to the bathroom. He then made his way downstairs to the kitchen, stubbing his toe on the coffee table on the way. He put on a pot of coffee, peeled a banana from the counter and ate it while he made his way back to the bathroom. He quickly shaved and showered, then threw on a pair of slacks and a button down shirt.

The phone rang. It was Detective Barton.

"Hey Steve"

"Hey."

"You up and motivated?" Barton asked with a bit of chipperness in his voice.

"Yeah... Getting dressed now"

"Good.Pick me up a pack of smokes on your way over to get me, will ya'?"
"Sure. Be there in a half hour."

"See ya."
They hung up.

Layton filled his large, stainless port-o-mug with coffee and dumped eight teaspoons of sugar into it. He stirred it with a butter knife from the dish drainer beside the sink and put the lid on it. He returned to the bedroom, retrieved his 9mm pistol and holster, clasped it to his belt, pulled on a rainproof coat and took a last look in the mirror before leaving.

Detective Barton was waiting outside on his porch when Layton arrived. He was dressed similarly to Layton, but wore a bulky bullet-proof vest under a black t-shirt. He also sported a wool weave blazer, instead of the larger, more cumbersome jacket that Layton wore. He stepped into the Explorer and shut the door. Layton didn't move the vehicle right away. He was focused on a 'Re-Elect Cagle for Sheriff' sign across the street in a neighbor's lawn. He stared at it for a few moments, and then turned to Barton, "You think he'll win?"

"Who?" Barton asked confusingly.

"The Sheriff. You think he'll get re-elected?"

"I don't know," Barton hesitated, and then continued "Not if we don't come up with something in this case...and fast"

"Yeah, I know." Layton put the vehicle in drive and headed for the station. The two didn't speak during the entire drive.

~~~~~~~~~

To both the Detectives' surprise, Agent Raney from the FBI was already at the station when they arrived. They both greeted him and the three men found an empty interrogation room to work in.

Agent Don Raney hardly looked like your stereotypical FBI Agent. He wasn't clean shaven, didn't wear a dark suit and aviator-style shades, and didn't boast a higher-than-mighty attitude. Actually, he came across more like a construction worker, with his rounded salt and pepper crew cut, blue jeans and a thick mustache extending to his jaw line. His demeanor was casual and nonchalant. He had a deep, gruff voice, but spoke intelligently.

Agent Raney placed an overstuffed, soft-sided
~~~~~~~~~

leather attaché case on the table in the center of the room, and removed a large stack of manila case files from it. He sat down in a chair on the far side of the table as the Detectives both sat down across from him. Detective Layton also placed a couple of similar-looking files on the table in front of himself as Barton laid a composition notebook and a pen in front of himself. Agent Raney spoke first, "These are the case files from two years ago... in Florida. I've put them in chronological order. That should make things easier for you two to catch up on the knowledge of these cases. As you can see, the files are quite extensive, so we should start reviewing them right away."

"Would you like a cup of coffee?" Barton asked the Agent, as he stood up to get himself one.

"Sure...two sugars please." Raney replied.

Barton then turned to Layton, "You ok?"

Layton held up his own mug and said he was fine. Barton left the room.

Layton reached over and picked up the first file on the Agent's stack and began to study it. "Let's get to it," he said with a hint of exasperation in his voice.

~ 12 ~

Around noon, when he awoke, Marcus called a buddy of his -- Chance. Chance lived with Charli and had been dating her for years. They were supposed to be getting married the next summer. Chance had always hated the fact that Charli was a dancer and had tried to get her to quit for years. He had met Charli (Lisa), before she had ever danced, when they lived in Central Florida. Lisa had always wanted to move to the mountains of North Carolina, and Chance loved her so much, he was willing to move there too, even though his ex-wife lived in Asheville. A few years ago they had made the move with Lisa's three children, whom he adored as if they were his own. Everything had been normal for about a year until Lisa came to him one day and stated she wanted to try dancing a couple of nights a week in a strip club. Chance had been outraged at the idea and had told her 'Absolutely Not!' However, within a few weeks, Lisa had made up her mind that she was going to dance, with or without his consent. Their relationship drastically down spiraled from that point on.

"Chance...hey... it's Marcus...What's going on?"

"Not much, Marcus. What are you up to?"

"About six-foot-five, ha ha," Marcus said jokingly.

"Very funny man," Chance replied, smiling into the phone.

"Just calling to see what you were up to these days, since you never call me anymore."

"Yeah, I know. Sorry, things have just been fucked up with Lisa lately, so I haven't much felt like doing anything."

"Sorry to hear that man. I know you love that girl, but I keep telling you to STAY AWAY FROM THE STRIPPERS!"

"I know, but you know she wasn't a stripper when I met her, Marcus," Chance replied defensively.

"But she is now, man, and you know as well as I do, that once they get into that life they never get out," Marcus reminded him.

"I know, but this is different. She--"

Marcus interrupted him, "No, it's not. There's nothing different. She dances, drinks like a fish, and is hooked on *the shit*. How is that different?"

"Well, because--"

Marcus interrupted Chance again, "Look man. I know strippers, and she's no different. Trust me!"

A sense of frustration came over Chance. He hated how blunt Marcus always was, but ultimately he knew that Marcus was right. 'He *was always right, when it came to women,*' he thought.

"Goddamnit, Marcus!"

"Hey, don't get mad at me, man!"
"I'm not mad. I just hate it when you're right... This time I wish you weren't."

Marcus's voice softened with sympathy, "I know man. I actually like Lisa, but she's wrong for you, man. You deserve better than her. She's gotten a taste of that life now, and she's changed, man. She'll never be that wonderful girl you met and fell in love with dude. Time to move on."

Chance's eyes filled with tears, "I know she's cheating on me too, Marcus."

"See man, she's worthless."

Chance tried to regain his composure as he wiped a tear from his cheek. He wanted to continue to defend her to Marcus, more to satisfy his own feelings than to actually convince Marcus that she could again be the sweet, kind, loving person he had fallen in love with. But again, he knew his efforts to revert her had become futile months ago.

"So, what's new with you, Marcus?" Chance said as he cleared his throat.

Marcus took the hint, "Nothing man. Just the same ole', same ole'."

"How's your daughter?"

"Still haven't been able to see her. That cunt ex of mine is still fucking me over on visitation," Marcus replied.

"Sorry to hear that."

"No biggie." Marcus tried to sound as if he wasn't upset.

"Well, good luck though."

"Thanks man, I really appreciate that." Marcus

quickly changed the subject, "Let's get together this week, buddy. I've got a couple of people I want you to meet."

"Sure, who?"

"Just a couple of hotties to take your mind off your winch."

"Don't call her that man!"

"Ok... sorry," Marcus chuckled.

"And, I won't cheat on Lisa either. You know that."

"Yeah, yeah. I know. No one said anything about cheating man. Just hang out with us. One of them is having a party Wednesday night."

"I don't think so."

"Why not? Live a little!"

"I am living," Chance retorted defensively.

"No you're not, man. That woman of yours is living! And she's got you all fucked up in the head."

"Yeah... and?"

"Don't be a pussy, man. I'll pick you up Wednesday at eight. Lisa will be gone to work by then, right?"

"Yeah, she leaves much earlier these days."

"Alright. See you then, man. Be cool."

"Yeah, okay. See ya'."

Marcus hung up first, while Chance just let the phone drop to his shoulder. He held it there as he dazed for a few moments, then closed his eyes, shook his head back and forth and wiped away another tear streaming down his cheek.

~~~~~~~~~

Detective Barton returned with a Styrofoam cup of coffee in each hand. He gave one to Agent Raney, and set one down on the table in front of himself. He lit a cigarette and offered one to the Agent.

"No thanks. Don't smoke," Raney said, as he waved off his offer.

"So, where do we start guys?" Barton asked
~~~~~~~~~

inquisitively.

"Your partner is reviewing the first case we had in Florida," Raney said as he pointed to the file in Detective Layton's hands.

"Here take a look at this." Layton held out the file for Detective Barton.

Barton took the manila folder and flipped through it briefly. He came across a crime scene photo page, as he began to sit down. At the site of the photo, his movement towards the chair slowed down dramatically. A look of disgust came across his face. As his rear hit the hard, metallic chair, his shoulders slouched and he raised his eyes to Agent Raney in disbelief.

"This is abominable!" He exclaimed with a grimacc on his facc.

"I know," The Agent responded.

Barton flipped through a few more photo pages before closing the file. His stomach was beginning to churn violently.

"So, how did this guy manage to elude you fellas?" Barton asked.

"He's a slick bastard. He's meticulous, and never leaves any evidence behind."

"Seven times? And your forensic lab couldn't find a damn thing?" Barton asked in disbelief.

"No. After the third time, we even started to think he might be a cop or an agent himself."

"And?"

"We eliminated that theory."

"Why?" Barton asked curiously.

"Well, one of our profilers said this wasn't the work of a cop. I didn't necessarily agree with her, but we were ordered to discontinue with any investigation regarding any law enforcement personnel," Raney explained.

"What about previous law enforcement officers?" Layton interjected.

"Not that either. Based on the profiler's description, she figured it was someone who was a 'fanatic' of police procedures. But most likely, someone who was 'rejected' for a law enforcement position at some time in their life, not an actual cop or agent.

"Did you follow up on that then?" Barton asked

"We couldn't. That's probably over thirty thousand people nationwide."

"But all the crimes took place in Brevard County right?"

"Yes?" Raney didn't seem to know where Barton's line of questioning was headed.

"So, did you check applications that were turned down shortly prior to the crimes, in that county, and surrounding ones?"

"Hmmm?" Raney coupled his chin in his hand as he thought back, and then continued, "I didn't personally, but we had over a dozen Agents working on this case. I'm sure someone did."

Agent Raney really wasn't sure that someone had done this research, but he didn't want the Detectives to know this. No Agent ever wanted to admit that 'The Agency' may have overlooked something in an investigation, *especially*to small town cops.

Layton continued to thumb through more files and then handed them to Barton. Agent Raney stood up and walked over to a window covered with steel mesh. He stared out the window at the drizzling rain as he pondered over the case in his head. He knew almost every single detail by heart. He had worked the case from day one and had re-reviewed the files and the crime scenes dozens of times over the last couple of years.

Raney and the two Detectives continued to compare files and exchange notes and theories throughout the day.

~ 13 ~

It was 7:30pm. The Club was quiet, as usual for a Monday night. Six dancers and only four customers. It had only been open a half hour as Scarlet approached the manager by the front door.

She was an enticing girl standing at almost 5'8", and nearing her 27th birthday. She had straight, dark brown hair that flowed all the way to her full, perfectly rounded ass. Her facial cheeks protruded like tangerines, and radiated a soft rosy color. She had dark brown, alluring eyes and epicurean lips. Her hips and thighs were thick, but were spared of cellulite dimples.

She threw on her obviously faked charm, cocked her head to one side, and batted her eyelashes as she asked the manager if she could go ahead and leave, since the club was so dead.

The manager looked at his watch briefly, took a quick glance around the room, and then told her it was okay for her to leave. She responded by bouncing up and down a little then kissed him on the cheek and thanked him with an ear-to-ear smile. She then made a military-styled about face, and gracefully made her way to the dressing room. She emerged twenty minutes later in a pair of faded blue jeans, a white t-shirt and flat-soled canvas shoes. Most of her makeup was removed and her hair was pulled up in a bun on top of her head. She said goodbye to a couple of other dancers on her way towards the front doors, then slung her duffle bag over her shoulder and left.

The temperature outside was about fifty degrees and the parking lot was full of puddles from the bitter-cold rain. The moon was full and the wind howled through the branches of the large Dogwood trees that surrounded the parking lot. The Bouncer walked Scarlet to her car and made sure to look in the back seat of her 89' Probe before allowing her to get in. She thanked him as she started the car. He shut her door and went back and stood under the baby blue canopy covering the front entrance to the club. He continued to watch her as he waited for her to allow the car heater to kick in. She put the car in gear and drove off, giving a quick wave to the Bouncer, as he went back into the club.

Scarlet followed the ramp onto the Interstate by-pass and headed west towards I-26. A truck followed about ten car lengths back, but she paid it little attention after first noticing it in her rear-view mirror. About five minutes onto I-26, she reached her exit. She followed the off-ramp to the bottom and turned into a convenient store and parked directly in front of the doors. The truck followed her down the off-ramp, but drove slowly past the store. As she exited her vehicle, she watched the red truck pass, but couldn't see the driver through the heavily tinted windows. A few moments later it was out of site and she entered the store to buy some cigarettes. She then returned to her car and drove the two miles to her apartment. As she pulled into the complex, she didn't notice the same red truck parked in a line of cars across from her building. She grabbed her duffle bag out of the back seat and headed up the stairs to her second story apartment. She fumbled with her keys for a moment then slid one into the lock. As she pushed the door open, a gloved hand suddenly reached around from behind her, covering her mouth. Her eyes widened in instinctual terror as she tried to scream, but only a silent muffled squeal could be heard. Her attacker quickly shoved her through the doorway and shut the door behind.

~~~~~~~~~~

Detective Layton continued to leaf through the stacks of case files as Detective Barton and Agent Raney
~~~~~~~~~~

used a dry erase board to compare similarities of the crime scenes. Layton had five folders opened to their crime scene photo pages and spread out across the table. He carefully looked at one, then another, and then another, until he had looked at all of them. He then started back at the first, repeating this over and over. He was looking for visual similarities between the crime scenes. All of a sudden, a mysterious look came across his face and he shuffled the files around to get a better look,

"Hey!" he exclaimed.

Barton and Raney both stopped what they were doing and glanced over at him.

"Come here," he said as he motioned to them.

They both came over to the table as Layton took a single step back, continuing to stare intensely at the scattered collage of photos.

"What is it?" Barton asked curiously.

"I think I found something...well...maybe," Layton said with half surety.

"What?" Raney asked.

"Look at these three photos." He pointed to three different ones, "Look at the sheets."

Barton and Raney both bent over the steel table and surveyed the photos.

"Do you see it?" Layton asked.

"See what?" the other two both asked simultaneously.

"The sheets! They're all silk...see?"

Barton glared intently at the photos, and then realized what Layton was referring to. Agent Raney picked up a photo to retrieve the Crime Scene Data Sheet from underneath it. He studied it for a moment as he followed his reading with his right forefinger.
"Actually, the crime scene report here says they are satin sheets." Raney corrected.
"Check the others" Layton said with a bit of urgency in his voice.

Agent Raney checked a couple, while Barton checked the rest.

"Yup, all these too. All of them are satin!" Barton sounded off.

"Same here," Raney informed them.

"Hmmm...coincidence?" Layton asked.

Raney responded, "I don't know. Maybe not."

"What about the cases where the attacks weren't in the bedrooms?" Barton asked Raney.

"From my recollection of all the scenes in Florida, I remember now, that all the victims did have satin sheets. I was at all the crime scenes and went through them with a fine-toothed comb. Yes, they did. I'm sure of it! What about your two crime scenes? Did they?"

Layton jogged his memory back to the bedroom in Swannanoa, then to the Candler scene, "Well I know for sure the Swannanoa attack did." He thought harder, going over images in his mind of the Candler case, "I can't be positive about the other one though. We found her hanging on her front door. I went through the bedroom that day, but honestly can't remember if there were satin sheets on the bed or not."

"I'd bet a twenty that there were." Raney said with confidence.   The three men looked at each other. They were all thinking the same thing, 'This *can't be a coincidence'*.   The atmosphere in the room changed quickly to that of urgency. Agent Raney spoke first, "We need to find out how these sheets tie into each crime. If they are the same brand, style, color, etc. Also, we need to find out where they were purchased and how long ago."

"Right. I'll re-interview the victims." Layton volunteered.

"I'll get the sheets we do have, from the evidence room and send them down to forensics again," Barton said as he picked up the telephone on the table.

Raney took his cell phone from his belt clip and dialed FBI headquarters in Jacksonville, FL to get the information from his people.

Pray For Death

~ 14 ~

About 11:00pm, a young, drunk couple playfully made their way through the gate to their apartment complex's swimming pool area. As they staggered their way to the outdoor Jacuzzi by the clubhouse, they awkwardly removed each others' clothing. After they were completely nude, they slowly slipped into the steamy hot tub with a bottle of champagne. They passed the bottle back and forth for a few minutes, gulping the bubbly liquid down their throats as if they were parched from a few days in the desert. The young girl finally took the black, rose-print covered bottle and set it on the edge of the Jacuzzi, then straddled her anxiously awaiting lover. Her nipples hardened as she slowly rode up and down on her partner's stiff erection. She kept her eyes closed, arms wrapped around his neck as she buried her face in his shoulder. She moaned softly as they continued for a little while, and then raised her head in anticipation of her own orgasm. She opened her eyes, and then froze. Her partner seemed slightly perturbed and looked up at her face. Noticing her vapid stare, he turned to see what she was zoning on.

Only a few yards away, sitting upright in a patio lawn chair, under the peach colored clubhouse awning, was a nude woman. Her hands and feet were duct taped to the arms and legs of the chair. She was unconscious. Her long, brown hair hung down over her left arm. Both her breasts had been sliced vertically down the middle, and her saline implants removed. Blood streamed from both incisions and flowed slowly down her stomach to her shaven crotch. Her left ring finger had also been severed off and thick red blood dripped down to the silvery satin sheet spread neatly underneath the chair.

~ 15 ~

Agent Raney's hotel room phone rang about 11:40pm. He was sitting at an oak wood desk intensely studying over the case files in a pair of blue, plaid boxers and a white undershirt when it startled him. He answered with a firm, businesslike tone, "Raney."

"This is Steve Layton," the voice said on the other end of the receiver.

"Yeah, what's up?"

"We got another one."

"Where?"

"In Arden, on the south side of town," Layton replied.

"Alive?"

"Yup, same MO. I'll pick you up in a few minutes."   Raney had already picked up his neatly laid out pants from the bed and was sliding them on as he answered, "Okay, I'll meet you in the lobby."

He hung up the receiver, put on a clean shirt from

the armoire, and made his way to the bathroom vanity. He turned on the cold water, cupped his hands under the faucet and splashed some water on his face.

Before drying his face, he leaned over, placed both hands on the counter top and stared deeply at his own reflection in the mirror. As he stared, an image of his ex-wife slowly faded into view behind him. She approached him lovingly, with a sensual smile on her face, and slid her hands onto his shoulders then down his arms and around his waist. She whispered 'I *love you Don*' a she playfully took a nibble at his ear. Raney pressed his eyes closed tight and shook his head once, then re-opened his eyes to see that she was gone.

Don Raney was born in 1963 and had been raised in Groton Long Point, a political subdivision of the town of Groton, on Long Island Sound in New London County, Connecticut.

His father had been a Navy Captain stationed at the United States Naval Submarine Base New London (the Country's first Naval Base), while his mother had been a professor at the Global Research and Development campus of Pfizer, Inc. He had been raised in public schools and had later attended Brigham Young University

(BYU) in Utah, receiving a BS in Accounting. He worked for the local police department back in Groton for two years before applying to the FBI. He had married Alison Baldwin, the Senior Class President and a Cheerleader, right after graduating with honors. Her family had contested their relationship from the beginning, as Don was not a Mormon. They had been married for 7 years and had tried to have children during this time, but after several miscarriages, they found out that Alison would never physically be able to do so. This news had caused her to fall into a deep depression that she hadn't yet recovered from. Don had had no choice but to institutionalize her in 1991 as she had become almost completely listless. He had hated to do so, but new it was the best thing for her. He visited her there, every weekend for ten years afterwards, but finally couldn't handle the stress anymore. She had become non-responsive to his presence, and the pain of this was tearing him apart.

~~~~~~~~~~

Detective Layton honked his horn once outside the lobby where Raney was fixing a cup of coffee. Raney immediately grabbed his coat and made his way to the Explorer. They drove silently for a few minutes before Agent Raney asked, "Another stripper I presume?"
~~~~~~~~~~

"I'm not sure yet. She was unconscious when she was found, so we haven't gotten a statement from her yet. Detective Barton is on his way to the hospital now to interview her."

"Who found her?"

"A couple of young lovers having a good time in the Jacuzzi."

"A Jacuzzi?"

"Yeah, it's an apartment complex with an outdoor one."

"She was found outdoors?" Raney seemed a bit puzzled.

"Yeah."

"That's odd. None of the other victims were found outside. It sounds like our boy is either getting bolder, or is trying to send a new message."

"Message?" Layton asked.

"Yes, there's obviously some deep rooted personal motivation behind these crimes A hatred of some kind, sparked either by the attacker's sexual inadequacies or some personal childhood trauma," Raney explained.

"Is that your theory or a profiler's?"

"Both, however, I'm not sure if it is necessarily a childhood trauma. It could be some sense of an adulthood rejection."

"That makes sense," Layton agreed.

Raney continued, "The attacker wants us to know that these attacks are personal to him, not random. There is more of a link between these crimes than just the fact that all the victims are strippers."

"What's the other link then?"

"That's what we need to find out. And when we do, we should be able to nail this bastard!"

They arrived at the scene a few minutes later. As usual, the place was swarming with cops and bystanders. Raney said he was going to take a look at where the victim was found, while Layton interviewed the couple who had found her.

Layton approached the pool area and ducked under the police tape. He asked a uniformed sergeant where the couple was, and was pointed in their direction.

He made his way over to them and glanced briefly at the lawn chair covered in blood, and the remnants of twisted duct tape, as he passed. He also noticed the satin sheet neatly laid out underneath it. He immediately knew that the attacker was now making sure the Investigators knew that the sheets were no coincidence. They were his signature for each of these crimes.

"Hi, I'm Detective Steve Layton," he said as he held his hand out to shake the young man's hand.

The young man shook his hand and introduced himself as Josh Love, then turned slightly towards the young girl standing next to him and introduced her as his girlfriend, Summer Stevenson.

Layton couldn't help but to notice how beautiful the young girl was as he softly shook her hand for an extended length of time. He was captivated by her radiant green eyes bordered by her long, dark, curly eyelashes. Her lips were sharp and streamlined and softly reflected the surrounding light. At their touch, the young girl smiled with obvious interest. As she did, her dimples took shape and only added to her sensuality.

Layton snapped out of his temporary daze, let go of her hand and asked, "So, you two found the girl, right?”

Josh took charge of the moment, attempting to alleviate the obvious attraction between his girlfriend and the Detective, “Yes, my *girlfriend* and I were *making love* in the hot tub, when she first noticed the girl in the chair. I then looked over and saw her too.”

Layton tried to stay focused on Josh, but couldn’t help periodically glancing over to the young girl wrapped in her towel.

“What time was that?” Layton asked.

“About 11:00pm, I think,” Josh replied as he twisted his lips and squinted his eyes in recollection.

Layton looked down at the champagne bottle still sitting next to the Jacuzzi and asked, “Is that yawls’?”

Summer replied softly with a smile, “Yes, I love champagne.” Her boyfriend quickly and defensively interjected, “We weren’t drunk, and we are on private property!”

“Relax kid. I wasn’t accusing you of anything. It’s my job to observe everything at a crime scene. Even though you both look too young to be drinking.” He shot a matter-of-fact look at Josh, then smiled and seductively glanced at Summer once again, but cut it short when her boyfriend threw her a harsh glare.

As Layton continued to question the young couple, Agent Raney surveyed the crime scene from every angle. He was now kneeling down to the sheet, gently and carefully flipping over the corners, looking for a tag. He spotted one and jotted down the information from it into a small spiral notepad. He then continued to canvas the area and take notes.

~~~~~~~~~

Detective Barton arrived at the hospital around midnight. He entered through the Emergency Room doors and briskly walked up to the male triage nurse sitting behind a small desk. He flashed his badge and asked to see 'the *girl just brought in with her finger severed off'*. He didn't mention the other wounds.

"She's in the OR, but you can't go in there," the nurse informed him.

"Is she critical?"

"No."
~~~~~~~~~

"I need to see her right away then," Barton urged.

"I'm sorry," the nurse continued with his lisp, "Not until the Doctor says it's okay."

The Detective slapped his hand down on the desk, causing the nurse to jump. He looked at the surprised face of the nurse for a moment then decided not to pursue his demands. He asked the nurse in an aggravated tone, to inform him immediately when the Doctor would allow him to see her.

The nurse's look turned to disgust as he agreed to do so.

Barton glanced around the room, and then went outside to smoke a cigarette. After lighting it, he pulled out his cell phone and called Detective Layton.

"Layton here."

"Yeah, it's Ken. I'm at the hospital."

"Find out anything?"

"No, she's in the operating room now, and they won't let me in there. I'm gonna' stick around til' they do, though. You got anything?"

"Not much, but our boy left his calling card again." Layton informed him.

"Satin sheets?"

"Yup, but this time the victim was found outside by the pool."

"Hmmm, that's different."

"Yeah. I'm interviewing the ones that found her and Agent Raney is collecting some evidence around the scene."

"Alright, I'll call you later. Oh, don't forget, we have that press conference in the morning."

"I know. We'll get together early tomorrow morning and prepare for it." Layton replied.

"Okay. I'll let you know if I get anything from the victim."

"Good." Layton hung up.

Layton and Raney wrapped up their investigation about 2:30 in the morning. Layton offered Raney to stay in his guest bedroom as they had to get an early start in the morning. Raney accepted the offer and the two went back to his place, but not before Layton caught Summer unattended by her boyfriend and slipped her his cell phone number.   Barton waited around the hospital until about 4:00am, before being allowed to speak to the victim.

Pray For Death

~ 16 ~

Although she danced under the name Scarlet at the club, her real name was Heather Dietz. She was an Asheville native from a middle-classed family. She was college educated, but had pursued a modeling career after graduating. She had become disappointed when she was continually turned down for modeling jobs because of her weight. She wasn't fat; however, the industry was currently using 'crack addict' thin women. She did a couple of department store catalog shoots, but had been unable to support herself long-term, so she turned to stripping. At first, she was shy and hated it, but the allure of so much cold hard cash soon changed all that. She never liked taking her top off, but she averaged $150-$200 a night, so she endured it. Her plan was to dance for three years, enough time to save the money to move to Hollywood, California and continue to pursue her modeling career. She only had six more months before she was going to make that happen.

~~~~~~~~~~

Barton went to the Intensive Care Unit where she was moved to and asked which room she was in, flashing his badge once again. He entered the room and quietly shut the door behind him. Heather was propped up in her
~~~~~~~~~~

hospital bed just staring straight ahead. She glanced over briefly at the Detective. He showed her his shield, and then she turned her head back forward.

"Hello, Heather," Barton said in as soft and comforting a voice as he could, "I'm Homicide Detective Ken Barton, with the Sheriff's Department.

Heather glanced back over at him with a confused look on her face, "Homicide?" she asked.

"Yes, but I'm temporarily assigned to our Sex Crimes Division."

"Sex crimes?" she asked, again sounding confused.

"Yes ma'am. The nature of these crimes makes them fall under that department's jurisdiction."

Barton took a few steps into the room and asked if he could sit in the chair next to the bed. She nodded an 'okay'. He sat down and fumbled in his coat pocket for his notepad and a pen. He seemed nervous and uncomfortable. It was no surprise that he was. Hell, he wasn't used to talking to the victims of the crimes he investigated. After all, he was a Homicide Detective.

After gathering basic information about her, he

began to question her about the attack. He couldn't help but stare at the large bandages wrapped around her chest and left hand.

He started, "Do you have any idea who did this to you?"

Heather paused for a moment, looking down at her chest, and then answered, "No", as she closed her eyes.

The Detective fidgeted in his seat and lightly tapped his pen point on his notepad. He wasn't sure exactly what to ask or how to ask it. He was also terrified of what her reactions might be. His eyes were heavy and his thoughts unclear from the long night, but he knew he had to finish while her recollection would be fresh in her mind. He continued to ask her questions about the attack and the attacker for about a half hour. By the time he was finished, she was sobbing and had turned her head away from him. He thanked her, wished her well and left the room, leaving his business card next to the bed. He stopped in the hall, just outside her door, as he composed himself and put away his notepad and pen. He rubbed his eyes gently then checked the time on the wall clock above the nurse's station. It was 5:40am. Just then, an orderly bumped into him, excused himself without looking up, and then went on his way down the hall. The Detective noticed a small folded up piece of paper and been dropped by the orderly. He picked it up, unfolded it and noticed it was a prescription sheet. On it, in red ink, was written:

'2 100ml Saline Implants'

The Detective quickly turned around and looked down the hallway for the orderly. He was nowhere in sight. Barton thought for a moment, 'Is *this the Doctor's order for implants to replace the victim's?*' He showed the prescription to a nurse at the station and asked her if that was how a Doctor would order such things. She replied, "Absolutely not!"

"Shit!" Barton exclaimed, "Goddamnit." He knew now that the attacker was fucking with him, and that the orderly could have been him. He hadn't even gotten a good look at his face. He looked once more down the hallway, then down at the paper in his hand, before he left.

~~~~~~~~~

When Detective Layton and Agent Raney arrived at the police station at 7:00am Tuesday morning,
~~~~~~~~~

numerous reporters were already in the press room setting up their equipment. Barton arrived a few minutes later. The conference wasn't to begin until 9:00am, so that gave the Sheriff and the three investigators about two hours to prepare. They all immediately went into the Sheriff's office and sat down. Sheriff Cagle was already at his desk with an open can of Skoal in front of him. He pinched some with his fingers and placed it between his lip and gums. Barton cringed a little at the site, while Layton lit up a smoke.

"Alright boys, you'd better have something for me!" Cagle barked in his usual stern, demanding voice.

Layton took a deep breath, then exhaled as he began, "Well sir, we still don't have any suspects, but that's not necessarily what we need to tell the press. We have however, come up with some leads."

He continued to tell the Sheriff about the satin sheets, their theory that the perp has some sort of medical and/or possible police training, and that he is taunting the Detectives by personally placing clues for them to find.

Overall, the Sheriff was not impressed with the status of the investigation and made this quite clear. Nevertheless, he had been dealing with the Press for many years, and knew how to manipulate and stretch the facts. It was always a bluff that could backfire, if results weren't eventually achieved, but Cagle had faith in his Detectives and was willing to gamble heavily on them. He excused the three men and began to prepare his short speech for the half dozen cameras awaiting his appearance in the room down the hall.

~ 17 ~

Charli rolled out of bed around 1:00pm on Wednesday afternoon, her usual time when she had worked the night before. Chance had left earlier that morning to open up the Ice Cream Shop they owned in the mall. She staggered to the bathroom, peed and brushed her teeth. She then fumbled around the mess of clothing next to her side of the bed, until she found a pair of black jeans. She reached into the front pocket and pulled out a small plastic bag filled with cocaine. She sat down, still naked, on the edge of the bed and pulled out a razor blade hidden in the top drawer of her night stand. She poured out some coke onto the stand and chopped at it for a few minutes. She reached into her wallet on the floor and retrieved a fifty dollar bill and tightly rolled it up. Using the bill, she snorted up the cocaine. Her eyes watered, causing her mascara to run down her face. She then put everything away and pulled out a vibrator from the night stand and lay back on the bed.

She and Chance hardly ever had sex anymore, because of their conflicting schedules, so she had gotten used to pleasuring herself. She slid one hand down her stomach and began massaging her clit with her middle finger as the cocaine rush began to hit her. Her other hand gently stroked her left nipple. She closed her eyes and gently bit her lower lip. She continued to rub her clit, every few moments sliding her finger inside herself, to moisten it. After a few minutes, she took the vibrator from next to her, turned it on, and placed it on her now swollen clit, as she aggressively fingered herself with her other hand. She continued until she had made herself cum twice. She had just put the vibrator back into the drawer, when she heard the front door opening. It was Chance. He came into the house and set his keys down on the kitchen table, then headed to the bedroom. Lisa had pulled the covers over herself and pretended to be asleep. Chance quietly walked around to her side of the bed and sat down on the edge. He held a single yellow rose in his left hand as he gently brushed her hair away from her face with his right. He caressed her cheek softly, "Hey baby, wake up," he whispered. She slowly opened her eyes, still pretending as though she had been sound asleep, but Chance knew better. He could see the traces of the white powder near the openings of her nostrils, and had already noticed some left on the bedside stand. He played along with her charade, though.

"Hey honey," she said as she stretched and groaned a little, a small smile creeping across her face, "What are you doing home?" she continued, as she glanced over at the alarm clock.

"I got Rebecca to come in to work early, so we could spend some time together before you went into work." He held up the rose for her to see.

Lisa scooted herself up to a sitting position and took the rose from his hand, "Thanks sweetie. It's beautiful, but, I'm leaving early today."

"Early? Why?" Chance asked as he felt a sense of loss come over him. He was used to it though.

Lisa always seemed to have an excuse as to why they couldn't spend any time together. "Jade is coming to pick me up in about an hour. We are going to get our nails done, do some shopping, and then go tan before work."

"Can't you cancel?" Chance asked demandingly.
"No baby, I promised her I'd go," Lisa replied, trying to sound sympathetic.

Chance became aggravated. "So, what's more important? That or me...us?"

"I'm sorry baby," Lisa tried to say in a consoling voice, even though she really wasn't sorry, "I promised." She turned and rolled across the bed and stood up on the other side. She pulled Chance's monogrammed terrycloth robe from the closet and headed towards the kitchen to put on a pot of coffee. Chance reluctantly followed.

Lisa fumbled through the cabinets in search of the coffee filters. Her search started out slow and calm, but became almost frantic as Chance continued to hound her about her priorities.

"Why do you do this all the time Lisa?"
"What?" she replied, keeping her back to him.

"Avoid me. That's what!"

"I don't avoid you!" Lisa was trying to sound sincere, but was failing miserably.

"Yes," he paused, "you do!"

"Whatever!" 'Whatever' was always Lisa's way of saying 'Fuck *You, I'm through with this conversation*'.

Chance knew this and decided not to push the issue. He just shook his head and retreated to the bedroom to lie down.

Lisa finally found the filters. They had been right in plain view, next to the coffee pot, the whole time. She sighed and proceeded to make a pot of coffee. She lit a cigarette and sat down at the kitchen table. She felt guilty, but allowed her selfishness to take charge. She drank the entire pot of coffee over the next half hour, and then headed to the shower. Chance observed her without moving his head from his blank, forward stare, following her only with his eyes. Nothing else was said.

Lisa showered, dressed and left when Jade honked the horn outside, never once looking at Chance.

~~~~~~~~~

Around 7:00pm, Chance awoke to the telephone ringing. He was still lying face up on the bed, fully clothed. It was Marcus.

"Hey man, you ready?"

"Ready for what?" Chance asked confusingly.

"The party, man. Remember?"

"Shit Marcus. I don't think I'm going to go." Chance replied solemnly.

"Fuck that! You're going, man, Or I'm gonna' kick your ass!" Marcus said in a stern, but playful manner.
~~~~~~~~~

"Really Marcus. I don't feel up to it." Chance pleaded.

"No, is not an option. Get dressed. I'll be by to pick you up in an hour." Marcus hung up.

Chance rolled his eyes, but couldn't help smiling. He knew Marcus only meant well, and was looking out for him as a friend. He held the receiver button down for a second, with his forefinger, then released it and dialed Lisa's sister's house. The sister's husband, Brad, answered.
"Hey Brad"

"Hey"

"How are the kids?" Chance asked, referring to Lisa's children. The children rode the bus each day to Brad and Tina's house after school, to play with their two boys. It was convenient for Chance and Lisa, since Chance was usually working when school let out and Lisa was never in any shape to pick them up at that hour. They usually stayed until about five o'clock, when Chance would leave the ice cream shop for the day to pick them up.

"They're fine," Brad informed him.
"Sorry I didn't come get them at five. I left work

early and took a nap. I just woke up."

"No problem."

"Actually, I was wondering if they could spend the night over there. Would that be a problem?" Chance asked.

"No, that's fine," Brad replied. He really didn't mind. He worked the third shift at Datapress, and Tina would be there to watch them.

"I appreciate that Brad," Chance continued, feeling as if he needed to explain why he had asked, "Lisa is working tonight, and I have something I've got to do. You sure it's okay?"

"Yeah, of course, Chance. You know we don't mind. Just drop off some clean clothes for them to wear to school tomorrow, before you go out."

"Sure, no problem. Let me talk to them for a second, though," Chance instructed.

"Hold on," Brad replied, as he called the kids away from the Nintendo.

Chance asked both the children how school was

that day, then asked if they minded staying at Aunt Tina's for the night. They loved staying there and excitedly said so. Chance told them he loved them, and reminded them to be good. He hung up the phone and took a quick shower, shaved and got dressed. He had a few minutes to spare before Marcus would arrive, so he pulled out a photo album and thumbed through pages of snapshots of himself, Lisa and the kids. He realized, now, that he had forever lost the woman of his dreams.

~ 18 ~

Marcus squealed into the driveway promptly at eight o'clock. He left the car running, jumped out and strode briskly to the door. He knocked heavily, just as Chance opened it.

"Let's go. You ready?" Marcus impatiently asked.

"Yeah. We just have to make a quick stop on the way."

"Sure, where?" Marcus asked.

"I need to drop off some clothes for the kids. They're at Lisa's sister's."

"Okay."

Chance grabbed a bag of clothes from the couch and locked the front door behind him on his way out. They both got into the car and Marcus squealed the tires down the road. A few miles later, they arrived at Tina's home in Enka, a small unincorporated town adjacent to Candler. Chance went to the door. It was open, except for the screen door. He said 'Hello' to the children through the screen and they immediately jumped up from watching Shrek on the television, and ran to the door. He opened it and gave them both a big hug. First, David, the 5 year old boy, then Jennifer, the 7 year old girl. The oldest girl wasn't there. A year earlier, she had moved to Alabama to live with her father. He spoke to them briefly, left the clothes, waved to Brad on the couch, and returned to the car. The children immediately retreated to their spots in front of the television.

Marcus once again squealed the tires as he headed towards the evening's entertainment. As they drove, Marcus asked, "What about this psycho, man?"

"What about him?"

"Aren't you worried about him?"

"Me?" Chance confusingly asked.

"No, man," Marcus chuckled, "Not you... Your girl. Aren't you worried about her?"

"Of course I am. I even tried to use that as another desperate excuse to get Lisa to quit dancing. But she's so goddamned stubborn. Just like her mother."

"She better be careful. This guy don't play!" Marcus added.

"I know. But the drugs have her thinking she's tougher than the world," Chanced replied. He didn't really want to spend the evening worried sick about it, so he changed the subject, "So, who are these chicks we're going to see?"

"Oh man, you're gonna' love these broads They're fine as shit!" Marcus exclaimed excitedly.

"Who are they, though?" Chance asked.

"Cindy and Katrina."

Knowing Marcus's reputation, Chance threw a glare at him, "Please tell me they're not Strippers!"

Marcus laughed, "No man... I promise they're not strippers!"

"Good!" Chance replied with a sigh of relief.

"Don't worry... all that matters is that they are fine, they love to party, and they are both into each other too."

"They're lesbians?"

"Well, actually, they're bisexual." Marcus clarified deviantly.

"Geezis Christ Marcus! What the hell are you getting me into?" Chance retorted as he rolled his eyes, not sure if he even wanted to continue the evening.

"Oh, fucking relax, man... You're hangin' with Marcus tonight... You know I wouldn't do you wrong."

Chance just cracked the window, lit a cigarette, and looked out into the darkness. Even though the thought of two women having sex was an exciting one, he could only think about Lisa, and how much he missed her affection.

The two drove for about five more minutes, until finally reaching their destination, about two miles from the airport. The house was a fairly modern three bedroom, two bath, brick ranch home in a well manicured neighborhood. Chance seemed a bit surprised when they pulled up to the house. It definitely wasn't what he had expected. Actually, he hadn't really expected anything in particular, but he was still a little taken back. About two dozen cars lined the driveway and the street out front.

Marcus found a spot under a large pine tree in the corner of the lawn and parked the car. They both exited the vehicle and walked towards the large, varnished oak front doors. A row of Tiki flame torches lit up both sides of the walkway. One of the front doors was cracked open and the two strolled into the marbled tiled foyer. The inside of the house was attractively decorated, from pastel colored walls and crown moldings, to fabulous modern artwork hanging throughout. Marcus seemed un-by the surroundings, as he had obviously been there many times before. However, Chance seemed in awe, as he took in the homes ambiance.

As they made their way into the living room, they were surrounded by dozens of thick, aromatic candles providing the lighting in each room. Marcus seemed to know just about everyone he passed. He shook hands, kissed and greeted them all. He introduced Chance to each of them as they moved throughout the house. About thirty to forty people, between the ages of twenty-one and forty, littered the house.

Chance noticed the women outnumbered the men, three to one. Under different circumstances, or during other times, this would have been an exciting situation for Chance, but despite the warm, sensual surroundings, Chance still couldn't fully relax and get Lisa off of his mind.

Marcus noticed how uncomfortable Chance

looked, so he instructed him to fix himself a drink at the bar in the corner of the room. Chance couldn't wait to get a screwdriver in his system to ease his tension. He nodded at Marcus's order and quickly made his way across the room to pour himself a few ounces of relaxation.

Marcus made his way through the rear sliding glass doors to the suspended, wooden deck out back. More Tiki torches lined the edges of the porch, creating a warm atmosphere in the chilly night. He immediately noticed the party's hostesses, Cindy and Katrina, and gave them both a sensual kiss on the lips. The two were roommates, as well as lovers... Marcus's kind of crowd.

Marcus grabbed a bottled water from the large cooler on the deck, "Hey girls... there's someone I want you to meet... he's a good guy... a little nervous... so be easy on him."

"Cool!" the two roommates said simultaneously, as they both smiled from ear to ear.

"Fresh meat," Katrina added with a raise of her eyebrows.

"Where is he?" Cindy asked, as she looked

around.

"At the bar. I told him to make himself a drink, to calm his nerves."

"Why's he nervous?" Cindy asked.

"He's in love," Marcus replied.

"He has a girlfriend?" Katrina asked.

"If you want to call the bitch that... She runs him over like a freight train, but he stays with her anyways... He just needs to realize that there is a softer world out there." Marcus squeezed Katrina's ass and smirked.

Katrina giggled, "We'll show him *soft*."

"Yup. After tonight he'll forget she even exists." Cindy added.

~~~~~~~~

Chance downed the first screwdriver in two large gulps and fixed himself another, then made his way to the back porch. As he crossed the living area, he noticed a sensual painting of a nude woman hanging above the fireplace. He eyeballed it with a look of approval as he continued across the room. Marcus saw him coming and
~~~~~~~~

yelled, "Chance!"

Chance turned to look at him, but it was too late. Chance's preoccupation caused him to run slam into the sliding glass door. He stood there stunned for a moment, and then realized his nose was bleeding. Cindy quickly grabbed a paper cocktail napkin and rushed to Chance's aid. She held the napkin tightly around his nose and tried not to laugh. Chance was embarrassed, but tried to hide it.

"I'm Cindy."

"I'm Chance," he mumbled back.

"Chase?"

"No, Chance!"

"Oh... Chance... cool name."

Marcus and Katrina rolled with laughter on the porch.

"Did I tell you he was nervous?" Marcus laughed.

"That's not funny, Marcus!" Cindy said in Chance's defense.

"Where's the restroom?" Chance managed to nasally wheeze, while Cindy continued to pinch his nose.

"I'll take you," Cindy offered, as she ushered him

in that direction.

A few minutes later, Cindy and Chance returned to the porch. Marcus was relaxed in a cushioned patio chair next to a large glass table, with Katrina snuggled on his lap. Chance pulled out a chair for Cindy, then at down in one next to her.

"You okay?" Marcus asked Chance.

"Yeah, I'm fine." Chance replied, trying to ward off Marcus's sarcastic concern, "It's nothing."

Cindy looked over at Chance and smiled softly. Marcus noticed she had obviously taken a liking to Chance. He smiled contently, feeling like 'Mr. Matchmaker'.

"We need some music," Katrina said, as she jumped up out of Marcus's lap. She went into the living room and put a CD into the stereo. Cindy got up and picked up Chance's empty glass from the table.

"I can get that," Chance said, as he sat forward and reached for the glass in her hand.   "No,   that's okay... I'll get you one." Cindy insisted.

Chance paused for a moment, and then relaxed

back into his seat, "Thank you," he said with a nod.

"You're welcome. Screwdriver, right?"

"Yes, thanks."

Cindy retreated inside the house.

"So what do you think?" Marcus asked Chance, after waiting for Cindy to disappear out of sight.

"About what?" Chance asked innocently.

"The girls, dummy!"

"Oh... yeah. They're okay." Chance said nonchalantly.

"Okay?" Marcus replied, surprised by Chance's seeming lack of interest, "What do you mean, okay?"

"What?"

"These bitches are fine as hell, and you say they're just okay?"

Chance glared at Marcus silently for a moment, and then looked down at his watch.

"Quit looking at your watch, man! You don't have

anywhere else to be."

"I know." Chance admitted.

"So relax. The night is young. Have some fun!" Marcus instructed.

Katrina returned to Marcus's lap, as Genesis' '*In The Air Tonight*' began playing through the mounted speakers on the side of the house. A surprised look came across Marcus's face and he turned his head to Katrina, "What the fuck is this?" he asked disappointedly.

"I like this!" Katrina replied defensively.

Marcus rolled his eyes, "How about some Outkast, or at least some Beyonce?"
"I *like* Phil Collins!" Chance interjected.

Marcus didn't acknowledge his comment as Katrina attempted to divert Marcus's attention by locking lips with his.

Chance *really* felt uncomfortable now. He took this opportunity to check out some of the other guest's faces... He didn't recognize anyone.

Cindy returned just then with a refill of Chance's drink and what looked to be a Purple Hooter for herself.

She handed him his glass, looked over at Katrina and Marcus, then reached down and took Chance by the hand, "Come on. Let me show you around."

Chance stood up. He was still uncomfortable with the whole setting, but figured nothing could be more so, than watching his friend make out. Cindy walked him into the house and took him on a short tour, never letting go of his hand. When they arrived at Cindy's bedroom doorway, Chance seemed a bit reluctant to enter. Cindy gave his arm a playful tug as she looked up at him and smiled.

Chance resisted, at first, but then followed her into the room.

Once inside, Cindy let go of his hand and coyly eyed him as she gracefully moved towards the bed. Chance took a swallow of his drink and nervously looked around the room. He was pretty sure what Cindy was up to. He'd been '*out of the game*' for a while, but could still recognize a squeeze play.

He sat down on the corner of the queen sized bed, as Cindy excused herself to the adjoining bathroom and shut the door behind her.

Chance thought momentarily of getting up and bolting out of there like a gazelle under attack by a cheetah, but his body just froze. He began to think about Lisa, but for some reason couldn't focus on anything good. Only bad recollections were storming through his mind. He shook his head vigorously, trying to clear his thoughts, but he couldn't shake away the scenes of Lisa's drug use, bad attitudes and her infidelity. He closed his eyes and poured the rest of his Screwdriver down his gullet. He reopened his eyes and decided to move himself to a Victorian styled love seat in the corner of the room. After doing so, he looked up, just as Katrina appeared in the bedroom doorway. He was surprised, but obviously Katrina wasn't. She threw him a seductive smile, and then continued into the room. Chance looked behind her expecting Marcus to appear, but there was no sign of him. Katrina slowly walked over to the bed, swiveled around and sat down. For the first time since meeting her, Chance actually looked her over. She was about twenty-five years old with long reddish-brown, wavy hair. She had a slender build and long silky legs. She wore a long, studded silk dress with a slit in the side up to her hip. Her skin was flawless and her 36C breasts rode slightly out the top of the v-line opening.

Chance could now feel the warmth of the alcohol

moving through his veins. He relaxed a bit, but remained silent as Cindy came out of the bathroom. Chance now looked *her* over too. He figured her to be about the same age as Katrina. She had shoulder-length, feathered, blonde hair and dimples on both cheeks. Her breasts were slightly larger and rounder shaped than Katrina's and her dark nipples shown through her white, lacy blouse. Although slightly shorter than Katrina, she had a much fuller shape.

Cindy glanced over at Chance and smiled innocently. She then made her way over to the stereo on the dresser and put on Kid Rock's version of '*Feel Like Makin' Love*'. Turning, she walked over and stood in front of Katrina. She crossed her arms in front of her body, grabbed a hold of the bottom of her blouse with both hands, and gently slid it over her head. Katrina immediately slid both of her hands up Cindy's stomach and began caressing her breasts. Chance shuffled his body to a more comfortable position in his seat as he watched Cindy's nipples harden to Katrina's touch. His heart began to beat rapidly - he couldn't believe this was really happening. Katrina leaned forward and began kissing Cindy's lower abdomen, just above her hip-hugger slacks. She glided her mouth slowly up to her belly button and playfully flicked its ring with her tongue. Cindy closed her eyes and rested her arms over Katrina's back, as Katrina unzipped Cindy's pants and slowly worked them off her hips, letting them drop gently to the floor. Cindy now stood there totally nude as Chance felt his blood rushing south.

Katrina lay back on the bed and slid her body towards the headboard. Cindy erotically climbed on the bed and straddled her thighs. She slid Katrina's silk dress up her body until she had it completely removed. Chance felt his penis swelling in anticipation. He got up, shut and locked the bedroom door, then returned to his perch. Neither of the girls even noticed as they wrapped their naked bodies around each other. From where Chance was sitting, he could see the moisture building up between both girls' legs. He was rock hard now and used every ounce of restraint in his body to keep from jumping onto the bed and ravaging both women. He wasn't even sure if thcy wantcd him to. '*Maybe they are just exhibitionists and wanted to put on a good show for him*', he thought.

Cindy was now going down on Katrina's wet vagina, licking and sucking on her swollen clit. Chance continued to watch in awe for a few minutes before Katrina turned to him and motioned for him to join them. That was all the invitation Chance needed. He had his clothes off in record time, and climbed into the middle of the love nest.

The girls took turns with their mouths on his large erect shaft as they continued to fondle each other. Then Cindy laid Chance back on the bed and climbed on top of him. She inserted his manhood into herself, and slowly rode him, while Katrina sucked on her nipples. A moment later, feeling a bit left out, Katrina straddled herself over Chance's face while she French kissed her female partner. The three continued their erotic encounter for over an hour, until they all collapsed from exhaustion.

Marcus made his way around the party, mingling with all the guests. He knew what the three were up to in the bedroom, and as he thought about it, a smile came across his face. He was genuinely happy for his buddy. Chance had been a rock for him over the last few years during his legal battles over his daughter... A true friend and Marcus valued his 'true' friends and would do anything for them. This was just his way of saying 'Thanks'.

Chance emerged from the bedroom first, with a sheisty grin on his face. Marcus noticed him immediately and called him over. Chance held up one finger to indicate that he would be there in a moment, and made his way over to the bar again. He made himself an extra strong drink, and then joined Marcus across the room.

Marcus looked at his face and chuckled. Chance turned red and shifted his eyes towards the floor.

"Have fun?" Marcus managed to get out between chuckles.

"What do you think?" Chance replied with a sarcastic smile.

"I'm sure you did, buddy!"

Chance couldn't get the smile to leave his face as Marcus patted him on the back, almost causing him to spill his drink.

"I'm sure they're not through with you yet," Marcus said with certainty.

Chance looked up from his drink in surprise, "Huh?"

Marcus just let out another chuckle and shoved a handful of peanuts into his mouth.

Just then, Chance's cell phone rang. He pulled it

off of his belt and read the Caller ID. It was Lisa.

"Shit!" he exclaimed.

"What?"

"It's Lisa."

Marcus reached for the phone, "Let me answer it," he said with a grin, and a raise of his eyebrows.

"Hell no!" Chance pulled the phone out of Marcus reach. He knew Marcus too well. He knew he would have loved the opportunity to fuck with Lisa's head. He'd never tell Lisa the truth about what was going on, but would have left Lisa wondering that something might have been.

"I'm going out front to answer it," Chance said, as he bolted for the front doors. He didn't want Lisa to hear the party going on in the background. As he passed through the front door, he answered the phone, "Hey baby, what's up?"
"Where the hell are you?" Lisa demanded.

"Out with Marcus, why?"

"Oh? Why didn't you tell me you were going out?"

Lisa's voice was agitated as usual, but this time Chance didn't cower. Instead, he put sternness into his voice and answered, "I didn't know I was going out. Marcus called and asked me if I wanted to get out of the house for a while, and I said yes."

"Where are the kids?" Lisa barked, changing the subject.
Chance made his voice even sterner,"They're fine. They're at your sister's for the night!"

Lisa changed the subject back, "So, where the hell are you?"

Chance felt a little bolder and figured now he would go ahead and tell her, "At a party."

Lisa was stunned and remained silent for a moment. Chance took this opportunity to wrap up the conversation, "I'll be home later... I'll see you when I get there.... gotta' go, bye." He hung up the phone and took in a deep breath. He realized this was the first time in their four year relationship that he had stood up to her. He blew out the breath, slowly, allowing his cheeks to fill with air. He took another sip from his drink, lit a cigarette, and went back inside. The smile from earlier came back to his face.

When he returned inside, he noticed that Cindy and Katrina had rejoined Marcus in the living room. He walked over and sat on the sofa next to Cindy. His cell phone rang again. He saw it was Lisa calling back and decided not to answer it. Cindy took a wild guess at who it was, "That your ole' lady?" she asked.

Chance looked at Marcus accusingly. Marcus just shrugged his shoulders and smiled. He now knew what they had probably been talking about when he had approached.

"Yes," he replied, feeling almost guilty admitting this fact to her.

"It's okay. We know all about her." Katrina admitted.

Instinctively Chance replied, "You do?" Then once again looked over at Marcus, who was pretending to look at something in another direction. Cindy scooted up next to Chance and leaned into him, making herself comfortable. She noticed Chance was a little bit stiff, so she took his arm and placed it around her shoulder. Katrina was already comfortable on the opposite sofa, leaning up against one of its arms, with her legs thrown over Marcus's lap. The four of them talked about a variety of mundane topics, keeping the mood light with laughter.

About an hour passed before Katrina whispered something into Marcus's ear. He smiled when she did, nodded a 'yes' to her, then immediately got up and took her by the hand as Journey was playing on the stereo. Chance figured the two of them were going to a room to have sex and gave Marcus a quick thumbs up. As they passed by the other sofa, Katrina reached down and grabbed Cindy's hand, playfully pulling her to her feet. Cindy, in turn, reached down and pulled Chance to his feet. Marcus led the four of them to Katrina's room. They stopped outside in the hallway, and Marcus ushered the girls in first.
Chance asked Marcus, "What's going on?"

"We're *all* going to have some fun now," Marcus replied with a big grin.

"All of us?" Chance replied shockingly.
"Yeah. Is that okay with you?"

"I... I... guess... but... no *fag shit*, right?" Chance asked worriedly.

"Of course not, dude!" Marcus replied assuredly.

"Okay then." Chance felt relieved. He had

actually been worried for a brief moment there. For the first time since knowing Marcus, he wondered about his sexual motives. 'Thank God!' he thought as he followed Marcus into the room and locked the door behind them.

~ 19 ~

Lisa arrived home from work about 4:00am. Chance had already showered and was watching television in bed. She showed her agitation, as she threw her keys down on the night stand and undressed. Chance didn't let it bother him like he usually did. He still had a good buzz going, and wasn't going to let her spoil it. Lisa jumped into the shower without saying a word to him. She planned to give him hell about going out, and for hanging up on her, but after thinking about it in the shower, she decided to use a little psychology on him instead. She knew that he had never turned down a sexual advancement from her in the past, so she decided she would be nice to him to see what his reaction would be. She thought this would let her know if he had been with someone that night. This is what she had thought all evening since he hung up on her, and it had been bothering her ever since. She got out of the shower a few minutes later and dried off. She thought about putting on a sexy negligee, but decided that would be a bit overboard. Instead, she wrapped her large cotton towel around herself, and lay on her side of the bed.

Chance took his attention away from the rerun of All In The Family, and asked how her night had gone.

She was still agitated, but hid it as best she could,

"Fine, and yours?" she replied.   "Great,"   Chance shot back at her, trying not to appear smug.

"You have fun?" she asked.

"Actually... *Yes I did*," he replied with a little arrogance creeping into his tone.

Lisa took the universal remote control from in-between them and hit 'Play'. The VCR came on, and she switched the television to channel 3. A porno was still left in the VCR from about a month before. The scene playing was of two women having sex with one guy. Chance couldn't help but to smile at the coincidence. Lisa noticed his smile but didn't acknowledge it. She knew that Chance really wasn't a big fan of pornographic movies, so she didn't know what to make of it. She, on the other hand, loved to watch them. Probably more than most people who like them. A few minutes into the video, Lisa reached over and began to caress Chance's penis through his boxer shorts. She noticed that he wasn't aroused, but knew that this wasn't uncommon. The videos never did anything for him. Chance really wasn't in the mood to have sex with her, partly due to the fact that he'd already had three orgasms that night. However, he figured that he'd better, so as not to arouse any suspicions. He set his mind to it, thinking about the events that had taken place earlier that evening, and within a minute he was ready to go at it. He climbed on top of her, without the usual extended foreplay. He fucked her hard and slow, never taking his mind off of Cindy and Katrina. Lisa pretended to be into it mentally, about as much as Chance. Physically she was playing the part, but her mind was obviously somewhere else. Normally, Chance was a great lover and almost always gave her multiple orgasms. But this time, she'd be lucky to get off even once. Surprisingly, the sex lasted almost fifteen minutes, and even without the foreplay, Lisa managed to have a fulfilling orgasm.

They climaxed together, and then Chance kissed her on the forehead and rolled back over to his side of the bed. He turned off the television, and then reached over in the darkness to caress her hand for a moment. "I love you sweetheart," he said with true sincerity, then rolled over and went to sleep.

Lisa didn't reply. She just rolled towards the outside of the bed and lay there, riddled with guilt. She *did* love him, very much so, but she felt like something was missing in her life. She didn't know what... just *something*. She nodded off to sleep as a tear streamed down her cheek.

Pray For Death

~ 20 ~

A couple of weeks passed without another attack. Detectives Layton and Barton almost seemed disappointed. They really weren't, but they both knew that criminals play an odds game the more they commit the crimes. Each time a crime was committed, it opened a potential possibility for the attacker to screw up and leave some sort of clue behind - A footprint, fingerprint, DNA, or a description embedded in the victim's memory. So far, this attacker had done none of the above, nor had he left any other clues... At least not any unintentional ones.

It was Thursday afternoon and the Sheriff was hard at work on the campaign trail. He had less than two weeks to convince the people of Buncombe County that he was still the man for the job. The Detectives and Agent Raney continued to pour over the evidence, looking for something that would lead them to the identity of the attacker. They were still no closer to solving this case than they were weeks ago and the frustration was taking its toll on them all.

Marcus was holding up his end of the bargain. He was frequenting Diamonds every few nights, observing everything and everyone he possibly could without being obvious. Although he hated strip clubs, he just continued to hope that Detective Layton would be able to assist him with his situation. In the end, he thought, that would make it all worthwhile. Unlike the majority of the customers, Marcus didn't spend much money on the dancers. Just a few $1 tips here and there, when the girls would take center stage. Mostly he just hustled on the pool tables in the secondary room, so as not to seem out of place. His winnings on the tables were averaging over $150 a night, making it seem worth his while anyhow. However, there was one glitch. Almost all of the thirty girls that worked there knew him well. They knew that he rarely ever came in the club when he wasn't selling the latest vibrator on the market. He hoped no one would question him about why he was now in there so often. So far, no one really seemed to pay it much attention, except Charli.

After the third time seeing him in the club in a week, she began to think that Chance had him spying on her. She had approached Marcus and made it known that she wasn't happy about it. Of course, Marcus denied the allegations, but Charli was convinced that Marcus was in Chance's pocket. Therefore, out of spite, she made sure that Marcus would have plenty to tell Chance, by hanging all over her customers, more so than what the job normally warranted. However, Marcus saw right through her charades and antics and paid it little attention. It really only made him despise her more than he already did. He had always loved strippers on a plutonic and business level, but had always hated them on a personal one. He thought they were all *'fucked up in the head.'*

~~~~~~~~~

About ten o'clock that evening, Marcus noticed Charli spending a considerable amount of time with one particular customer. This was not unusual, but Marcus just got a bad feeling about this one. The customer never smiled and really didn't seem like he was having a good time. Marcus kept a watchful eye on the two of them and noticed the guy never took his eyes off of Charli, no matter where she went in the club. At one point she went to the dressing room and Marcus noticed the guy just looking around the room nervously until she returned. It was only 11:15pm, and to Marcus's surprise, Charli had changed her clothes for the fourth time that evening. However, this time she wasn't in one of her sexy work outfits. She had come out in a sweat suit, with a duffel bag thrown over her shoulder.

Marcus wondered why she was leaving so early.

As Charli walked past the nervous fellow still sitting at a table in the middle of the room, she tried not to be obvious as she waved her hand at waist level, motioning for him to follow. The man waited a few
~~~~~~~~~

moments, until Charli had made her way to the front door, then he nervously glanced around the room once more and got up. Marcus continued to watch him as he made his way to the front door and left. Charli had already gone out into the parking lot.

Marcus said a quick 'goodbye' to his opponent, who was re-racking the balls on the pool table, and followed the two outside. He stayed back a ways, so as not to be noticed, as he watched Charli pulling out of the parking lot in her Trans Am. He noticed she was alone, but saw a grey Jeep Cherokee, with dark tinted windows, tailing her. He figured it was the guy that had followed her from inside the club. He jumped in his car and followed them up the street. He tailed them for about 5 minutes, noticing them exiting the expressway towards Woodfin, a small town a few miles north of Asheville. He continued to follow them to a small apartment complex on the west side of town. The two vehicles parked next to each other in the lot. Lisa exited her car first and walked casually over to the Cherokee. The man got out of his vehicle and once again nervously looked around before making his way towards the building. Marcus had swung his car into a parking space out of their sight, but was still able to see both of them. The two walked up a flight of outdoor steps and entered the first apartment on the left.

Marcus's first instinctual thought was to call his buddy, Chance, and let him know what was going on. As he held his cell phone in his hand, he thought better of it. He decided he *would* tell Chance, but not right away. He knew that Chance would confront her on it and it wouldn't take much for her to piece together where the information came from. This would screw everything up between himself and the Detective. He hated not being able to tell his friend, but his daughter came first and he didn't want to risk his chance to fix his situation with her. He reluctantly put down his phone, pulled out a pen and a piece of scratch paper from his glove compartment, and wrote down the address of the apartment. He then left for home.

~ 21 ~

Chance had stayed home that evening. His relationship with Lisa over the last few weeks had not improved a bit. That morning, at the Ice Cream Shop, he had decided he couldn't go on like that anymore and had decided he was going to leave her. After putting the kids to bed around eight o'clock, he sat down at the kitchen table and wrote her a letter:

- *My Dearest Lisa,*

I cannot go on like this, without you loving me. I have loved you since the moment I laid eyes on you. Never in my wildest dreams could I have ever imagined that a love like this could have ever existed. You filled the void in my life like the final piece to a puzzle. You are my soul mate, my love, my world. Just looking into your beautiful eyes makes me forget to breath. You are the most beautiful woman in the world and I cannot bear the thought of another man touching you. You are sacred to me, and I tremble at the mere thought of someone else holding you in their arms.

I touch your skin and my knees become weak. I kiss your lips and I feel faint. I wrap my arms around you at night and I truly believe I am in heaven. I smell your hair and I tingle all over. Countless nights I have

lay awake and watched you sleep so peacefully, watching you chest rise and fall with every breath you'd take.

I was such a fool to let you slip away from me. God knows I didn't mean to. I know now that I will pay for that mistake for all of eternity. I would have laid down my life for you without even the slightest of hesitation. Now, my heart and soul are empty. The only woman I ever truly loved is gone, and without you I am nothing, and have nothing. I will carry these wounds in my heart forever.

I truly believe that you loved me with all of your heart, at one time. I even believe that you still do. I believe that you are even "In Love" with me still. I think you have just masked it with bitterness. You are also fooled and blinded by the facade that someone else has created. It gives you a temporary fulfillment, as I once did. I can understand your need for that temporary "story- book" feeling, but by the time that you realize the difference between that and the "True Love" that we shared, it will be too late. When all the "freshness" and "serenity" fades away, and it will, one thing will still remain. That one thing will be "Our True Love" - An undying love that reaches deep into our hearts. But it seems now that you have gotten a taste of the

"Temptation" and are blinded by its deceptiveness. I truly do wish that you could "see through it" and search your heart and soul once again to find what I know is still there. But, it seems you can't, or won't.

Just know this, and never for a moment doubt my love for you - No one will ever love you as much as I do, nor with near the same intensity. My heart will always belong to you, and only you. You will always be my True Love. I wish you all the joy and happiness in life and I hope you find whatever it is in life that you are looking for. I just wish that you could have realized that it was lying right next to you. I am "setting you free"; for I feel that I have no other choice. My heart is broken and it seems as though it shall remain that way.

I Love You with All of My Heart and Soul...

~ Chance

After finishing the letter and wiping the tears away from his cheeks, he laid it on her pillow, grabbed his 2 large already packed travel bags, and woke the children. When they were both dressed, he dropped them off at their Aunt and Uncle's house and left.

Pray For Death

~ 22 ~

It was now late October and the weather had changed dramatically in Asheville. The temperatures during the day had dropped to an average of 45 degrees with the nights down in the lower 30's. The Flu Virus this year had hit harder than usual and was spreading like wildfire throughout the area.

Detective Layton watched the 6 o'clock news broadcast at McGuire's Bar and Grill on Tunnel Road. He relaxed in a booth with a Michelob Light and a dozen hot wings. The bar was nothing fancy, but had been in business for over thirty years, making it somewhat of a landmark in the area. A few years back, under a new law that had passed, it had become a private club, forcing them to sell $3 memberships to new patrons. It also required a three day waiting period before each membership became active. A law that Buncombe County enacted, intended to keep a spontaneous drinker from having a place to randomly stop for a nightcap.

The bar had two pool tables, a jukebox, a foosball table, three video poker machines and a couple of bar top video games scattered throughout its 2,000 square feet of dimly lit space. It also had a small kitchen serving mostly fried foods and appetizers to their customers, making up only about 20 percent of their gross sales. The other 80 percent was taken in through beer, wine and liquor sales to the hundreds of loyal patrons who frequented the establishment regularly.

Detective Layton coughed a few times. He hoped he wasn't coming down with the Flu, but figured it was likely. He glanced up at the television above the bar just as a Special Report by Darcel Grimes came across the screen - '*Terror in Asheville*!' flashed up on the set as Darcel began reporting about the '*rash of attacks*' on females in the area. Layton sighed in disgust. He hated the Press and the way they distorted the facts to make headlines. Throughout the broadcast, Darcel failed to mention that the attacks were *only*on Exotic Dancers. Her failure to mention this important fact would most likely cause an unnecessary panic among many women in the area who needn't be worried.

Layton finished his wings and took a final swig of his beer before paying his tab and leaving. He was on his way to the airport to pick up his brother, sister-in-law and their four small children. They were coming for their annual visit, and Layton was dreading every moment of their five day stay. Normally, he looked forward to it, but this year he was stressed about this particular case, and really just needed the quiet time.

He arrived at the Asheville Regional Airport at 7:15. As he pulled up to the passenger loading area, he spotted his sister-in-law, Katie, on the curb. She waved for his attention and he pulled in-between two taxicabs. His brother, Sean, came out of the terminal with the four children in tow. Steve helped Katie load the kids into the Explorer first, while Sean started loading the ridiculous amount of luggage into the back. Steve then helped him with the last few bags and they all exchanged hugs and kisses.

The fifteen minute drive to the house seemed like an eternity. The kids were wild and loud with excitement and made sure that there was no chance of the three adults being able to carry on a conversation. The oldest child, Damon, was four, followed by his twin three year old sisters, Tiffany and Tara. The youngest child, Nathan, was only sixteen months. Layton knew this was just a taste of what was to come. He loved the children, but could feel his blood pressure rising rapidly. '*Deep breaths, deep breaths... in and out... in and out*' he kept repeating in his head. It was going to be a long week.

After settling into the house and putting the children to bed, the adults relaxed in the living room. Steve made everyone a drink from the bar, while Sean built a fire in the fireplace. The three settled in and laughed and joked late into the evening.

~~~~~~~~

Steve and Sean only saw each other one time a year, but spent most of this time together making fun of current events and celebrities, instead of catching up on each other's lives. They were both extremely light-hearted comics, but lived stressful lives all year, so they always used this time as a tension reliever. It was actually good therapy for Steve. He rarely smiled all year, let alone bust out in tear jerking laughter. His brother was actually quite talented. He could impersonate over forty different celebrity voices and always had an unlimited supply of new jokes with each visit. Steve had always tried to persuade Sean into using his talents to land a job in the entertainment industry, but Sean personally never thought that he was good enough. He had had stage fright since he was in grade school, but still loved to practice his talents in private. Although, eight years earlier, he had landed a job at Universal Studios in his hometown of Orlando, Florida, he now worked as a waiter at a local chain restaurant with his wife. They struggled to make ends meet, but they were happy. Their family was the most important thing in their lives and they always made sure the children came first.

Unexpectedly, Katie broke the light atmosphere, "Steve, what's the story with this slasher?"

Steve had hoped they weren't going to bring up
~~~~~~~~

the case, but knew it would probably surface sooner or later.

"What have you heard about it?" he asked.

"It's been all over the national news," Sean explained, then continued, "They report on it

constantly."
"Yeah, we even saw some video footage of you a few times," Katie added.
"Of me?" Steve seemed surprised as he pointed at his own chest.

"Uh huh... They had some shots of you entering a crime scene and that short interview you did with Channel 13," Sean said as he got up to refill his drink.

"I don't pay much attention to the news," Steve admitted, "They usually distort everything anyhow."

"So, what's the status? Any leads? Suspects?" Katie asked with intrigue, as she sat forward in her seat.

"This guy is good. He's really putting us through the ringer on this one," Steve replied.

"Do you have any idea who it is?"

"Not yet, but I think we're getting closer." Steve said in his own defense.

Suddenly he felt like he was being hounded by the Press. He hated not having any suspects or solid leads. He was a good Detective and he knew it, but this case was really putting him to the test. Not only testing him as a Detective, but also his ability to cope with stress. He had never drunk so much until this case had been assigned to him. Some days he felt he could pull all his hair out.

"This is stuff you expect to hear about in a big city, like Miami or L.A." Sean said, as he leaned up against the fireplace mantle, "Stuff like this isn't supposed to happen in rural places like this."

"Asheville isn't so rural anymore," Steve corrected, "Crime is low, per capita, but definitely not obsolete. We have our fair share of rapes, murders and more. But drug abuse is probably our biggest problem here."

"Like Cocaine and Heroin?" Katie still seemed excited, like a reporter on her first big story.

"No, actually, we have more of a Rush Limbaugh epidemic around here."

The three laughed.

"Really? Prescription drug abuse is your biggest crime?" Sean asked in disbelief.

"Actually, yes." "Wow!" Katie exclaimed.

Sean loved that his brother was a Detective. He thought it was so cool. He used this opportunity to ask if he could assist in any way with the investigation. Steve was hesitant in offering to allow Sean to assist, but his brother was persistent in offering his services, "Hey, even if it's just a little, I'd love to be involved," Sean pleaded.

Steve agreed to review some of the case with him, but really didn't know how his brother could be of any formal help. Katie felt like her interest in the case had been tossed aside, so she made sure to make Steve promise to include her as well. He promised, and then excused himself to bed, explaining that he had to work in the morning. They all said their 'goodnights' and Steve graciously told them to help themselves to anything they wanted. Sean and Katie thanked him and snuggled into the couch to watch Saturday Night Live.

~~~~~~~~~

Steve awoke several times throughout the night to
~~~~~~~~~

the sound of Nathan crying. Each time, he heard someone go to the kitchen to heat up a bottle in the microwave, then make their way back to their own room. Always, within five minutes, all was quiet again, but the interruptions to Steve's sleep would assure that tomorrow would be a long day. Each time, he repositioned his pillow over his head to drown out the noise.

Before he wished it to, the alarm clock on the bedside stand sent out its familiar head rattling buzz. Steve rolled over and slammed down the snooze button, hoping to catch another fifteen minutes of much needed sleep. He wasn't going to get it. Within a minute, two curly haired twins were slapping their pudgy little hands up and down on his back. It startled him at first and he slid his hand quickly underneath his pillow to his awaiting 9mm pistol. Before pulling it out, he realized who they were and gently rolled over to give them both a hug. Tiffany told him he *looked like doo doo* in her squeaky little voice and Tara agreed with her. They both ran out of the room screaming at the top of their lungs. Steve rolled over and popped a couple of Tylenol into his mouth, then realized that he had nothing to wash them down with. Just then, Katie knocked on the doorframe and held up an offering of steaming coffee, "Lots of sugar, I remember," she said, obviously impressed with herself.

Steve made sure his lower half was covered by the bed comforter and motioned her in, as he sat up. She handed him the coffee mug and he took an oversized sip to wash down the pain medicine. After swallowing, he gasped and fanned his tongue with his free hand, attempting to cool his now burning mouth. Katie giggled and left the room, passing Sean in the doorway.

"Hey Goober!" His brother playfully greeted him.

Steve responded with, "Hey Goober," in a similar tone.

'Goober' was a nickname they had both called each other since boyhood. For some unknown, odd reason, they had continued it into adulthood. They both chuckled a bit as Sean aggressively slung open the bedroom curtains, blinding Steve with the morning sunlight.

"Geezis," Steve whimpered, as he covered his eyes with the back of his hand.

"Get up," Sean blurted, "Time to catch The Ripper!" He continued in his usual playful manner.

Steve put his hand down, allowing his pupils to dilate to a comfortable level. He threw Sean a look as if to say '*You're a Dork*!" before educating his over-eager brother, "He doesn't *kill* his victims."

"Whatever," Sean replied, not caring that his analogy hadn't been accurate, "Let's try to catch this freak!" He replied, as he squinted one eye and used his fingers to pretend as if he was firing a pistol.

Steve just rolled his eyes upward at his brother's antics.

"You wantin' to go to the office with me today?" Steve asked, figuring that was probably what was on his brother's mind.

Sean pretended as though he hadn't had that intention, but immediately volunteered his services. He told Steve he'd be ready in ten minutes, and then exited the room for a chance to gloat to his wife about getting to play Detective for the day.

Steve set his coffee down next to the bed, scratched the whiskers on his neck, and then forced himself to start his morning grooming routine.

Thirty minutes later, dressed in his usual work attire, Steve made his rounds with the children. He kissed and squeezed them playfully, then kissed Katie on the cheek and instructed his brother to get in the car. Sean responded with his Joe Pesci, Lethal Weapon impersonation, "Do I get a gun? Huh? Do I?"

Steve knew which scene he was re-enacting and completed it with a firm "No!" They both laughed as Sean kissed his wife goodbye and the two left.

A few miles down the road, Sean impersonated Sean Connery, asking, "Aren't we going to get some doughnuts?"

Steve had gotten used to his brother's impersonations over the years. He had to. His brother did one about every thirty minutes when they were together. Sometimes he even did them back to back. Steve used to think it was annoying, but he had become accustomed to it over the years.

His brother had always been a cut up, just like himself. However, Steve had changed over the ten years he'd been a cop. He still loved to act silly, but without his brother around, he rarely found the opportunities to do so. Being with his brother reminded him how much he missed him.

A few blocks later, Steve pulled into a fancy

looking Bakery and Doughnut Shop in the Biltmore Village. Sean realized where they were and let out a burst of laughter. The two went inside and joined the service line. When it was their turn to order, Sean asked for one glazed, one chocolate éclair, two jelly filled donuts and a regular coffee. The obviously gay cashier smugly told him that they didn't serve 'regular' coffee there. They only served '*exotic blends*' and sarcastically proceeded to name off a few.

"We have Brazilian Chocolate, Hungarian Herb, Dark Columbian Roast, Mediterranean Mint–"

Sean obviously couldn't stand this little punk and interrupted him right then with an impersonation of Chris Farley from Saturday Night Live. He grabbed his belt with both hands and yelled "Well La-Dee- Friggen'-Da!"

The faggot wasn't amused as he cocked his head to one side, with as fierce a look as he could muster up. He placed one hand on his hip and handed Sean an empty cup, "Get whatever you want," he said with his stereotypical lisp, as he pointed to the row of air pots on the counter, "Next!"

The two brothers took their orders to go, and continued on to the Police Station. When they arrived,

Sean saw an opportunity, once again, to show off his talents, doing mostly actors who had played police roles in hit T.V. shows and films. They included Sylvester Stallone, Colombo, Arnold Schwarzenegger, Clint Eastwood and more.

Each person or group of persons that Steve introduced him to seemed to spark another voice. By the time they had reached Steve's desk, the entire station was rolling with laughter.

'*That's my bro*,' Steve thought as he smiled and shook his head slightly back and forth.

~ 23 ~

That morning, Sheriff Cagle was his usual pleasant self. He sat in his office, with the blinds open, eyes glued to the morning news. A local reporter was standing in front of a still smoldering, burned out trailer home, talking about the hazards of kerosene heaters. Detective Layton told his brother to follow him as he weaved through the sea of desks between his and the Sheriff's office. He knocked on the glass door. The Sheriff motioned for him to enter without taking his eyes off of the television. Detective Layton opened the door and held it while he ushered his brother in first. He looked at Sean and put his finger to his lips, indicating for him to be silent. The news report changed topics to a story about a City of Asheville raid on a puppy breeding farm. Sheriff Cagle muted the television set and turned to the Detective.

"Good morning, sir," Layton said, trying to sound slightly cheerful.

"Mornin'," the Sheriff greeted back in his usual gruff voice.

Detective Layton then introduced his brother to the Sheriff, "You remember my brother Sean, don't you, sir?"

"Yeah, of course," the Sheriff replied, as he nodded his head and shook Sean's hand, "Have a seat." He pointed to one of the seats in front of his desk. The two sat down.

"How's that lovely wife of yours, Betty Joe?" Sean asked.

"She's fine, thanks for asking...and your wife and kids?"

"They're great," Sean answered.

"You gonna ride with Steve today?" the Sheriff asked, as he reached in to the bottom file drawer of his desk and pulled out a sheet of paper.

"Yeah... thought I'd help him catch this modern day Zodiac Killer," Sean added.

Detective Layton looked at Sean, realizing another poor comparison of crimes. The Sheriff didn't seem fazed by Sean's attempted humor. He handed the sheet of paper across the desk to him, "You know the drill. Fill out the Liability Release Form before you go."

Sean took the form, grabbed a pen out of the caddy on the Sheriff's desk and began filling it out.

Detective Layton started talking about what each investigator was currently working on when Sheriff Cagle saw something on the news and hushed him. Cagle picked up the remote and un-muted the set. A newscaster was comparing percentages in a popularity poll in the campaign for the Sheriff's Office. Cagle was trailing his opponent, Joel Yager by 8%.

Detective Layton watched as the Sheriff's eyes sank in disappointment. Cagle shut the television off and threw the remote down onto his desk. Layton took this as a cue to leave. He stood up, tapped his brother on the shoulder and motioned for him to hurry up. Sean signed the bottom of the form and told the Sheriff to have a good day, as he handed the paper across the desk. The Sheriff just nodded in response and pulled out his can of Skoal, while the brothers left the office.

Waiting outside were Detective Barton and Agent Raney. Steve introduced his brother to each of the men. They exchanged greetings. Layton informed the men that he was meeting with an informant today and would meet back up with them that evening. Agent Raney responded with their plans to question the medical personnel and other staff members at the hospital.

Steve then took his brother into the locker room and handed him a bullet proof vest from one of the tall grey lockers, "Put this on," he instructed.

Sean held out the vest at arm's-, turning it back and forth as if attempting to figure out which side was the front. Steve reached over and turned it to the proper position, then turned to search through the locker for his reserve pistol. When he spun back around, he noticed that Sean had slid the vest over the top of his shirt.

"Is this right, Sarge?" Sean said comically in Gomer Pile's voice.

Steve responded with, "You've been watching too much Reno 911!" He continued, "It goes under your shirt, Dork!"

"I knew that, Sarge," Sean continued in the same voice, "I was just testing you." They both laughed as Sean fixed the vest.

A serious look came over Steve's face moments later, "On a serious not though..." He extended a small .380 caliber pistol; grip first, towards his brother, "I want you to carry this." He placed the gun firmly in Sean's hand.

His brother looked surprised as he surveyed the pistol in his hand, "Hey, I was only kidding when I asked if I could have a gun," he said as he extended the gun back towards Steve.

Steve put his hand up to stop the return, "No, really, I think you should hold on to that today... The guy we are after is no saint... He's already killed one cop, and I don't think he'd hesitate to do it again."

All of a sudden, his cheerful brother seemed a bit nervous when the reality of what was Steve was saying seemed to sink in.

"You do remember how to use one of these, don't you?" Steve asked, as Sean still stood there staring at the pistol in his hand.

His brother snapped out of his frozen state and replied, "Yes... I remember," as he checked the safety and slid the pistol into his belt. The two were silent for a moment, and then Steve turned and closed the locker door. He spun the combination dial and the two left the station.

Pray For Death

~ 24 ~

Charli hadn't gone to work for three days since Chance had left. She'd just been moping around the house in his robe, wondering if he was even going to call. He hadn't, and the reality of his absence was beginning to hit her. As she sat at the kitchen table, an overflowing ashtray in front of her, she began to cry. It was a soft cry at first, as the tears began to stream down her face. Then, like a dam breaking, her emotions came crashing through and she began to sob harder than ever before. Chance's letter was laid out on the table. She picked it up with both hands as a cigarette dangled in between the fingers of her left hand. Her hands were trembling as she reread parts of the note to herself.

"Why?... Why did I let this happen? Why was I such a fool?" she muttered in a low, tear filled whisper, as she continued to review his loving words.

Instinctively, she laid the letter down and got up from the table making her way to the cupboard above the sink. She pulled out a bottle of Absolute Vodka and fixed herself a screwdriver with some orange juice from the fridge. She returned to the table, with her drink, and sat down. She wiped her tears away with the thick sleeve of the robe and stared down at the insulting liquid. She stirred it with her forefinger for a few moments, then put her finger into her mouth and gently sucked off the fluid. She thought briefly about pouring the drink out in the sink and quitting drinking altogether, but as the tears began to well in her eyes again, she knew that this was her easiest escape. She took another look at Chance's letter, and then began to drink her sorrow away. By mid-afternoon, she was tanked. An empty carton of orange juice and a few sips of vodka were all that was left on the table. Chance's letter had found its way to the floor. She staggered to the shower, turned the water on and sat under the stream with his robe still on. She began to sob again.

~ 25 ~

Detective Barton and Agent Raney introduced themselves to the Hospital Administrator. They briefly explained why they were there and the Administrator told them to feel free to interview whomever they needed to. He also offered his own assistance with anything they might need.

The investigators began their questioning with the orderlies who were on duty, then moved on to the nurses, doctors and array of other hospital employees. Among other things, they asked for voluntary handwriting samples to compare to the prescription note in Detective Barton's possession. It was a long, painstaking task that would keep them busy for days to come.

Meanwhile, Detective Layton and his brother were having lunch with Marcus in a quiet, out of the way, Greek restaurant in Black Mountain. Marcus didn't have much to report, except the incident where Charli had left with a customer. He didn't tell the Detective that he had followed them and written down the address, because he didn't think it was pertinent to the investigation. That was information that he was saving for his buddy, Chance. He did, however, notice that Detective Layton seemed a bit agitated by the news. Sean also noticed the drastic change in his brother's attitude after he found out this information. Neither one confronted him on it though.

Marcus also mentioned that Charli hadn't been back to work since that night either. Detective Layton thanked Marcus and paid for the meal. Marcus left in his usual hasty manner, while the brothers finished their iced teas.

After leaving the restaurant, the two drove back down Highway 70, towards Asheville. Steve was unusually quiet and Sean didn't interrupt the silence.

Steve pulled into a convenience store and parked. He handed a twenty dollar bill to Sean and asked him to go inside and get a pack of cigarettes and a couple of sodas. He watched his brother through the rear-view mirror until he had entered the store. He then got out of the vehicle and dialed a number on his cell phone. It rang four times as he tapped his foot impatiently and stared at the front door of the store. Charli finally answered, "Hello," she said as she stood naked, soaking wet from the long shower.

Layton could tell she had been crying by the sniffles through the receiver, "Hey, it's me," he said in a comforting tone.

"Hey Steve."

"What's the matter?" Steve asked with concern.

"Chance left me."

There was silence for a moment, and then Steve asked, "When?"

"A few days ago," Charli answered as she flopped on to the bed.

Steve tried to continue to sound concerned, but really didn't give a shit. He hated to hear her upset, but surely saw this as a good opportunity for him.

"Geezis, Charli... I'm sorry... Are you alright?"

Charli began to cry again, "I don't... I don't know... And today is my birthday," she managed to get out between the sounds of her sorrow.

Steve looked up and saw his brother walking towards the Explorer. God he hoped he wouldn't come over to where he was standing. *'Please just get in the car... please,'* he thought. Sean held up two Mountain Dew bottles in one hand and a pack of Marlboro Lights in the other as if celebrating a victory. He reached the passenger side of the SUV and climbed in. Steve let out a sigh of relief, and then focused his attention back to Charli.

"Do you want me to come by tonight?" he asked, hoping the answer would be 'Yes'.

"Sure."

"What time?"

"It doesn't matter. Any time is fine," She sniffled.

"Okay, I'll be by around eight o'clock... Oh, and *Happy Birthday*."

"Thanks, Steve," she replied in a low muffle.
Steve hung up and climbed back into the driver's seat of the Explorer. Sean handed him a soda and his cigarettes, then turned forward and took a sip of his own.

"Ahem, Ahem," Steve held out his hand, palm up, across the center console.

"What?" Sean laughed

"My change," Steve directed

Sean stared at him blankly for a moment then did his best Austin Powers impersonation, "Groovy man, I almost forgot."

Steve rolled his eyes and continued to wait for his change before starting the vehicle. Sean gave in and the two continued on their way.

~~~~~~~~~

Their next stop was WalMart, to check satin sheet brands and styles. The manager of the store was a large, burly man with a Danny Devito hair style. He wore a white, short sleeved, pin-striped shirt, brown polyester slacks and a wide brown tie that fell short of his belt line by at least four inches.

As he led Detective Layton and his brother down the aisles to the bedding department, Sean had to stop and play with almost everything. He picked up a stuffed dog and imitated Triumph The Comic Insult Dog, drawing a small audience. Detective Layton and the Manager paused momentarily, and then continued on through the long maze of stocked shelves, until they reached the rear corner of the store. The Detective immediately began searching through the many styles and colors of sheets, looking for some that matched the ones found at the crime scenes. The Manager received a page over the intercom and excused himself.
~~~~~~~~~

Sean continued to entertain his now intrigued crowd of about ten people. He did a half dozen or so impersonations using whatever props he could find handy. The Manager passed by him on his way back to the front of the store and just smiled.

After about ten minutes of searching, Detective Layton hadn't found any sheets that matched the ones from the crime scenes. He quickly checked a couple of adjoining isles to make sure there were no more, and then made his way back to find his brother. When he found him, he noticed about a dozen people were on looking from the adjacent isle as well. Detective Layton smirked and shook his head from side to side as he approached the amateur show. He placed a hand on his brother's shoulder and waved off the crowd with the other, "Show's over, folks... Show's over," he said as he took a Kermit the Frog puppet from Sean's hand and stuffed it back onto the shelf.

"Same time next week!" his brother playfully yelled at the crowd as they dispersed.

Steve cocked an amused grin at him as he put his hand on his back and lightly shoved him towards the front of the store.

"You find what you were looking for?" Sean asked.

"No," Steve replied in a discouraged voice, "I thought you were here to help me."

"I was helping!"

Steve raised an eyebrow, "How?"

"Crowd control!" Sean replied with a burst of laughter.

Steve rolled his eyes, "Come on. We've got more stores to check."

As the two walked between the checkout lanes, Sean noticed a few folks who had been part of his audience. He raised one arm at a time and parade waved at them with a big smile.

Steve started to realize that his brother seemed to have gotten over most of his stage fright. Maybe he would try again to persuade him to pursue his talents; he thought as they crossed the parking lot and got into his SUV.

They stopped at a couple of small retail stores on

their way to Kmart. Steve made his brother stay in the vehicle, as he knew it would take twice as long if his brother came in with him. Sean reluctantly agreed to stay put.

Just before arriving at Kmart, Steve's cell phone rang in the console. Sean picked it up and read the calling number off out loud. Not recognizing the number, Steve shrugged his shoulders.

"Steve's Taxi Service," Sean said as he answered the phone.

"Hello?" A young girl's voice said confusingly.

"Hello... Who's this?" Sean asked.

"Is Steve there?" the voice replied, still confused.

"Can I ask who's calling?" Sean asked as he lowered his voice in a business-like tone.

"It's Summer."

"Summer?" Sean repeated out loud as he looked over at his brother.

Steve instantly realized who it was and snapped his fingers, holding out his hand for the cell phone.

Sean handed it to him.

"Hi," Steve said with a bit of surprised enthusiasm.

"For a second there, I thought I had the wrong number... Steve's Taxi Service?"

"That was just my brother fooling around. Sorry about that," he said as he looked over at his brother beating on the dash, as if he was playing the drums to the beat of the song on the radio.

Sean was too preoccupied to even notice his brother's piercing stare.

"So how are you?" Steve asked.

"I'm good."

"Not too frightened over that girl, are you?"

"No... I was rattled a bit at first, for a few days, but I'm okay now."

"Glad to hear that."

"So, have you caught the guy yet?" Summer asked.

"No, not yet... but hopefully soon." Steve replied.

"I hope you do. We don't need a psycho like that running around town!"

"No, we don't."

"Well... anyways... the reason I called is, I was wondering if you maybe wanted to do something tonight... You know, like catch a movie or something." Summer said with a bit of hesitation in her voice, sounding more like shyness.

'Shit,' Steve thought as he remembered that he was supposed to go over to Charli's that night.

"What time?" he asked, hoping it would be late. He figured he could go over to Charli's a little earlier than planned, and then meet up with Summer later.

"Well, I have to go by my Mom's house around eight, so I thought anytime around ten o'clock would be good. I think there are some late movies that start around ten-thirty or so."

"That sounds great." Layton was already undressing Summer in his head. He remembered how beautiful she had looked standing there, half-naked, in her thong panties and bra the night he had met her. A towel had covered most of her, but he had caught a few glimpses of her flawless body each time she had intentionally lifted the large beach towel on her shoulders.

"What about your boyfriend?" he asked as he suddenly remembered about Josh.

"Josh?... Don't worry about Josh. I just see him casually. He thinks he's going to marry me, but that isn't going to happen."

"Oh... Okay," Steve responded. He was taken aback by the situation, because he wasn't used to the carefree attitudes people had about relationships these days.

"I'll call you around nine and give you directions."

"Sure... talk to you then."

Steve pressed the 'End' button on his phone and set it back in the console. He was surprised that Summer had called. She was all of twenty-three, and he had ten years on her. Not that that mattered. It just surprised him that she would have had any true interest in him. He thought for a second, 'Maybe it's not a true interest... Maybe she's just a sex addict'. He grinned as he realized that was not a bad thing.

After checking Kmart and a few other smaller stores, Steve and his brother headed for home.

"That's it?" Sean asked disappointedly.

"Yup... For today at least. It's not all glitz, glamour and action like Miami Vice."

"Yeah... I see that," Sean replied, still seeming a bit disappointed. He reached into his belt and retrieved the pistol his brother had given him and asked what he should do with it. Steve told him to just place it in the glove box for now. Sean checked the safety, then opened the compartment in front of him and placed the pistol inside. He shut the hinged door then reached in the center compartment and read the titles on the CDs inside. He pulled one out and slid it into the stereo. He pushed the 'Skip' button until he reached his desired song, and then raised the volume as Kid Rock began singing 'You Never Met A Motherfucker Quite Like Me'. The two sang along to the words, keeping the beat with their entire bodies.

~~~~~~~~

They arrived at the house around 7pm. Katie and the kids were gone. She had left a short note on the kitchen table, 'Took the kids to Taco Bell. Will bring back some home for you guys. Love ya, Katie'. Steve read it first then handed it to Sean and looked at his watch, 'Damn,' he thought, 'It's getting late'. He excused himself and headed for the shower. On his way, he used the phone in the bedroom to call Charli. There was no answer. After his shower he tried once more to reach her by telephone, while he dressed. There was still no answer. Steve hoped she hadn't forgotten about their plans.

Katie arrived about seven-thirty with her entourage of screaming and crying children. Sean helped her get the food and kids to the kitchen. Steve followed them. Katie told them to 'help themselves,' as she pointed to the bags of food on the table. Steve thanked her, but told her that he had plans for the evening and would probably be eating out. Katie could smell his cologne filling the room and looked surprised, "You have a date?" she asked.

"Well, sorta'," Steve said, hoping she wouldn't inquire any further.

"Wow!" Katie looked over at Sean as she placed one of the twins in a chair, "Good for you... You need to get out and date. How long has it been? Three–"
~~~~~~~~

Sean cut her off just then, knowing that Katie wouldn't mean to upset his brother, but probably would, "Good for you, Goober... Have fun!" He gave Katie a look to ensure her silence.

Steve told them he would probably be late and not to wait up, then left.

~ 26 ~

On the way to Charli's, he tried to call her several times from his cell phone. She still didn't answer and he began to think that she had forgotten about their plans. He suddenly remembered that Charli had mentioned it was her birthday, so he swung into the mall to pick up a bottle of perfume. When he came out, he noticed it was 8:15pm. He called Charli's number one last time... Still no answer.

He was discouraged about not being able to reach her and briefly contemplated calling off the evening and just waiting for Summer to call. He stood outside of the mall entrance for a moment, then decided to go ahead over to Charli's, since it was only a few blocks away. He arrived at her door at 8:25pm. As he pulled into the driveway, he noticed a grey Jeep Cherokee parked next to her Trans Am. He pulled into the grass next to the vehicles and sat there for a second. 'Shit, I *bet she forgot and has someone else over*,' he thought as he sat there in the dark.

He glanced up at the front door and noticed it was slightly opened. He took a deep breath, exhaled, then got out of the car. '*What the hell would it hurt*,' he thought.

He figured if she was with someone else, he could

play it off as just a social call to drop off the gift. He reached the door and knocked lightly. There was no answer. He knocked again... Still no answer. He pushed the door open about halfway with his foot and peered in.

"Hello," he called out rather softly. He raised his voice a bit, "Lisa?"

He heard a loud thump, then the shuffling of feet down the hall towards the bedroom, but no one answered. Instinctively, he now pulled out his pistol from his shoulder holster and entered the house.

"Charli?" he called out. Still no response.

He slowly made his way down the hallway towards the master bedroom. The house was dark, except for a crack of light coming out from under the master bedroom door at the end of the hall. He crept quietly towards the shut door.

'BAMM!' Steve felt his head hit the wall as someone slammed their body into his from a side doorway. The fierce impact stunned him and he dropped his gun. He struggled to stay on his feet as he felt something come crashing down on the top of his head and shatter. He fell to the floor. He immediately tried to clear his head and get back to his feet, but the room was spinning and he couldn't get his bearings. Blood began trickling down his face as he heard someone running down the hallway back towards the foyer area by the front door. He knew he had to get up. He steadied his balance by placing his hands on the hallway walls and made it back to his feet. His head was throbbing as the hallway seemed to sway back and forth. He wiped the blood from his eyes and looked around the floor for his pistol. Although the hallway was dark, he spotted it through the haze in his eyes, and bent down to pick it up. He grabbed it with his right hand and staggered back down the hall towards the front door, steadying himself on the hallway walls with his left hand. Just as he reached the wide-opened front door and stumbled into its frame, he heard a vehicle start. Then someone squealed backwards into the street. It was the grey Cherokee.

He still couldn't see clearly, but raised his gun towards the fleeing vehicle and fired three shots. The Cherokee fishtailed around and sped off down the street. Steve lowered his smoking pistol to his side.

'Charli!' he thought with horror. He immediately staggered back down the hallway and swung open the master bedroom door.

On the bed, lying naked, face up and unconscious, on a set of black satin sheets, was Charli. Her hands and feet were tied to the large cherry wood sleigh bed and she was gagged. He approached her to check for wounds. The only thing he saw was a lot of blood running down her vagina. He looked closer at the bloody area and noticed her wound had been stitched up.

~~~~~~~~~

Steve followed the ambulance to the hospital. He arrived at the same time and screeched to a halt in front of the Emergency Room entrance. He left his vehicle double parked and frantically followed the two EMTs wheeling Charli into the Hospital on a gurney.

Charli was still unconscious as they urgently wheeled her into a small room. Doctors and nurses scurried in every direction. One nurse saw Detective Layton's bloodied face and stopped to check his head wound, and then told him to have a seat, and that someone would be with him shortly.

The Detective's head was still throbbing and the noises around him seemed a distant echo. He looked around the chaotic scene, but couldn't seem to focus on anything in particular. His sight became blurry again and
~~~~~~~~~

the room began to spin. Before he could locate a chair to sit down in, his eyes rolled back in his head and he fainted.

~~~~~~~~~

Detective Layton's cell phone sounded off and vibrated across the night stand. He slowly opened his eyes from his prone position on the bed. As his vision cleared, he realized that he was in his own bedroom; however, he couldn't remember how he had gotten there. He attempted to rise up to a sitting position, but couldn't. His bandaged head began to throb. He lay back down on the pillows and listened to his cell phone ring again, then listened as it stopped and the room became quiet. He lay there for a moment, attempting to recollect his memories. He didn't even know what day it was. He turned his head to look at the time on the alarm clock... It read 3:45am. He shut his eyes and immediately fell back asleep.
~~~~~~~~~

~ 27 ~

Two days had passed since the attack on Charli. She was lying in her Hospital bed around 8:00am, watching and old Jerry Lewis film, when Detective Barton knocked on the door. He waited a moment for a response, but didn't get one. He knocked again as he cracked open the door and peered in. When he saw that Charli was decently covered, he entered.

Charli looked over at him as he approached her bedside. Barton softly introduced himself.

"Where's Steve?" she immediately asked in response.

Although Detective Barton was surprised that she called him 'Steve', instead of 'Detective Layton', he didn't show it, "He's fine. He's at home," he replied, as he slid a chair closer to the bed and sat down, "You okay?"

"Not really," Charli answered in a fading voice.

Detective Barton knew what she meant by her response and now almost felt embarrassed by what had seemed to him to be a sympathetic question. "Can I ask you a few questions?" he asked softly.   "Sure,"

Charli replied as she picked up the television remote at her side and pressed the 'Mute' button.

Once again, Detective Barton was in the uncomfortable position of having to interview a victim of this sort. His nervousness showed through the sweat forming on his brow, and his fidgety hands.

Routinely, he pulled out his small spiral notebook and a pen, and prepared himself to ask Charli a series of personal questions. It was times like these he wished he had pursued a career as an Architect, like his father.

He dazed for a moment as he reflected on memories dating back to around the time he graduated High School in 1982. He remembered how he and his father had fought profusely about his refusal to attend college, and his desire to become a Police Officer. He recalled a particular argument they had in the living room of his parent's upscale home. It had almost turned into a knock-down-drag- out fight.

He snapped out of his daze moments later to find Charli staring at him. Her face concerned and puzzled.

"Are you okay?" she asked

"Ummm... Yeah... I'm O...kay." He regained his

thoughts about questioning Charli and began the ritual.

~~~~~~~~~~

Meanwhile, Sheriff Cagle stood in front of his tall floor mirror, straightening his police uniform to military perfection, making sure to cover the Devil Dog Marine Corps tattoo on his left upper arm by tugging slightly on his sleeve.

He was preparing to cast his own ballot today for the county election.

Betty Joe was busy in the kitchen making pancakes and scrambled eggs, Buster's favorite. She called out to him to let him know they were ready, but there was no reply.

Buster heard her, but was lost in thought. This was the first time in ten elections that he was actually worried about losing. He stared deeply at his reflection in the mirror, studying the wrinkles and grey hairs that Betty Joe said 'Gave him distinction'.

'Am I too old for this shit anymore? Should I have thrown in the towel this time?' He was thinking.

He sucked his gut in as he held his breath for a few moments, then exhaustingly released the air from his
~~~~~~~~~~

lungs, allowing his stomach to bulge back out, "Never! Never Surrender!" he confidently whispered out loud as he squinted his eyes into the mirror, "Never," his voice faded.

He grabbed his Stetson Sheriff's hat, placed it firmly on his head, about faced, and made his way downstairs to the kitchen.

~ **28** ~

Marcus sped up to Detective Layton's house and squealed into the driveway, almost rear-ending Layton's vehicle. He shut off the motor and jumped out. He briskly made his way to the front doors and rang the bell -- 'Ding Doong Dang Dong, Dang Doong Ding Dang'

As he listened to the long, drawn out bell, he grumbled out loud, "Uppity Bastard."

Layton heard the door bell in his sleep. It sounded like it was the bells of Notre Dame Cathedral, and he was standing directly under them. He reluctantly opened his eyes and focused on his surroundings.

'Ding Doong Dang Dong, Dang Doong Ding Dang' the bell sounded off again.

"Geezis Christ already... I'm coming," he muttered as he rolled out of bed and threw on his robe.

He tied the robe closed as he made his way down the stairs towards the front door. As he reached the bottom of the staircase, he realized his head was still bandaged, causing a look of confusion to come across his face. He continued to make his way across the foyer and unlocked the front door. As he opened it, the sunlight blinded him and he couldn't make out who the visitor was.

"About fuckin' time!" he heard a voice say. He recognized it immediately and asked, "What are you doing here, Marcus?"

Marcus took a step forward towards Layton. His large muscular body now blocking the sunlight from Layton's eyes.

"Heard you ran into some trouble," Marcus replied, "From the looks of your head, I guess the Intel I got was accurate."

Layton raised his left hand towards the bandage on his head, "Yeah... Seems–"

Marcus cut him off, "You gonna let me in or what?"

"Yeah, Sure... Come in," Layton replied as he stepped aside.

Marcus immediately turned and walked past him into the foyer. Once inside, he stopped to survey the house, "Nice place, man... Just wondering how a cop affords a nice fuckin' pad like this."

"Not that it's any of your business, but my wife was an attorney," Layton replied irratatedly.

"Well, that explains it!"

"Why are you here?" Layton demanded.

Marcus turned slightly and walked into the living room as he responded, "I got some info for you, man."

Layton followed him into the room and asked, "Okay, what do you have?"

Marcus stared up at an odd looking painting on the wall, "Is that one of those Booty Chelly things?"

"It's Bo...ti...chell...ee... and... no, that's a Picasso."

"Picasso? Who the fuck is that?"

Layton was becoming agitated as his head began thumping, "What do you have, Marcus!" he firmly stated, trying to get Marcus back to the point of his visit.

"Alright man, relax!" Marcus flopped down on a leather sofa. He paused for a moment as he ran both of his hands across its cushions in obvious admiration, "I heard about Charli."

"And?"

"I remembered that I didn't mention something to you the other day when we spoke."

Layton seemed to be growing more and more agitated by the moment, "What?" he almost hollered.

Marcus scratched the side of his mouth, "Well..." Marcus paused.

"Just fucking tell me what it is, Marcus!"

"Okay, okay. Relax, man. Wow, you need a Valium or something? I got some in the car if you want." Marcus said sarcastically.

Layton rolled his eyes. He flopped on to the loveseat across the room and buried his face in one hand.

Marcus continued, "Alright. The other night I was at the club and I saw Charli when she left."

"And?" Layton didn't look up.

"Well, she didn't leave alone. Well, actually, she did leave alone...technically. But a customer left at the same time, and they seemed to have had it prearranged."

Layton looked up with interest now and asked, "Was it her boyfriend?"

"Chance?" Marcus asked.

"Yeah. Chance!"

"No. It was some other dude."

Layton hesitated for a moment in thought and then asked, "You know who it was?"

"No," Marcus replied.

"You sure?"

"Yeah, man. I'm sure."

"Had you seen this guy before?"

"No...Never."

"Well, why the fuck didn't you tell me this before?" Layton growled.

Marcus became defensive, "I didn't think it was important."

"Important!" Layton yelled, "Geezis fucking Christ, Marcus! There's a psycho going around attacking strippers. I ask you to watch the club for anything out of the ordinary, and you didn't think that that was out of the ordinary?"

Marcus yelled back, "Fuck, man! No… I didn't think that was out of the ordinary. They're fucking strippers! That's what fuckin' strippers do. They meet their customers outside of work all the time!"

Layton shut his eyes and rubbed the bridge of his nose. His voice changed to a slow, controlled tone, "So why did you think it was important now?"

"Cuz' of what just happened to Charli. I don't know if that dude had anything to do with it, but I just thought I should tell you."

"Do you remember what this guy looked like?" Layton asked.

"Sorta'. It was dark, and I didn't get a good look at him."

"Okay, so… what do you remember about him?" Layton asked.

"Well, he was about five foot seven, one hundred thirty to one hundred fifty pounds. He had a beer gut and a goatee. Oh, and he was kinda' balding, too."

"Is that it?" Layton replied with disappointment.

"Fuck, man. You're that goddamn Detective. Not me. That's what I fuckin' remember!" Marcus belted back.

The two sat there silently for a few moments while Layton tried to keep himself from verbally attacking Marcus.

Eventually Marcus broke the silence, "I gotta' go to the hospital to see Charli."

Layton looked up with surprise, "You know her personally?" He asked.

"Yeah, of course I know her...and Chance."

Marcus replied, "I know all those strippers. But I am also pretty good friends with Chance, so I know Charli a bit better than most of the others."

"Why am I not surprised?" Layton responded with a cockeyed grin and a roll of his eyes.

"Let me ask you a question," Layton paused and then continued, "So...what is it exactly, that you hustle to these girls?"

Marcus took a deep breath, then exhaled as he leaned back against the back of the sofa and crossed his left leg over the other, "I sell them toys and shit."

"And shit?" Layton immediately asked.

"Yeah...shit... like videos, accessories and stuff."

"Porn?" Layton asked in an affirming tone.

"Yeah."

"And what the hell would accessories be?" Layton asked with a light chuckle in his voice.

Marcus shifted in his seat and switched to his right leg crossing the left.

"Bedroom accessories...you know...leather, gags, handcuffs and stuff."

"Oh," Layton tried to act surprised at the answer even though he had figured that was what accessories had meant, "I see."

"It's legal stuff, man," Marcus defensively replied, "It's not stolen or anything!"

"I'm sure it isn't, but that still doesn't necessarily

make it legal," Layton assured him, "You know, biz licenses, taxes, etc."

"Hey man, you gonna bust my balls here?"

"No...no I'm not...so, you make any decent money doing that shit?"

Marcus looked at him condescendingly, "Ummm...you see my car, my clothes, don't you. What do you think?"

Layton just tightened his lips and slightly nodded his head up and down.

Marcus rose up out of his seat, "There is one more thing."

Layton stood up, "Yeah, what?"

"I followed the dude home."

Layton looked slightly confused, "Who?"

"The guy, the one Charli left with."

"You...You what? Geezis' fuckin' Christ Marcus. You're an asshole!" Layton yelled, "Shit, you know where this motherfucker lives and you didn't say so before!... Goddamnit Marcus!"

"Well, fuck man. We don't know this guy is the one who did this shit," Marcus yelled back.

"Yeah, but we don't know he isn't either. So where the fuck does he live?"

"He lives in Woodfin," Marcus replied, lowering his voice.

"Where?"

"Mountain View Apartments."

"Fuck! I gotta' call my partner...Marcus I'll talk to you later...Oh, you know which apartment?"

"Yeah, 215."

"Goddamn, you are an asshole, Marcus!"

Marcus sarcastically replied, "Glad I could be of fuckin' service!... I'm outta' here...Later."

Marcus made his way to the front door as Layton picked up the phone on the end table and dialed Barton's cell phone number. He could hear the squeal of Marcus's tires, just as Barton's voicemail answered.

"Fuck," he said out loud as he waited for the beep. He left an urgent message for Barton to call him back, but didn't say why. His mind was already turning as to what his next step would be. He hung up the receiver and began to collect his thoughts together.

~~~~~~~~~~

Steve surveyed the living room and noticed a child's set of blocks on the floor near the coffee table. "Shit," he thought, "Where the hell is Sean?"

He stood up and made his way upstairs to the guest bedroom they had been staying in. Their suitcases were still there. He felt confused again. 'God I wish I could fucking remem–'

His thought was cut short by the sound of the front door opening and a set of keys jingling, then voices...It was them. Sounded like the whole crew too. He started down the stairs and saw Katie first. She was bent over at the bottom of the steps taking off Nathan's shoes. She looked up and noticed him coming down the stairs.

"Hey, Steve. You're up." She yelled to Sean in the kitchen, "Honey, your brother's up!"

"You feelin' alright?" she asked Steve as she
~~~~~~~~~~

noticed the pale, confused look on his face.

"Sort of," He responded, "A little dazed. What day is it?"

"Thursday," Sean replied as he rounded the corner, "It's Thursday, Goober."

As Steve reached the bottom of the stairs, one of the twins tugged on his pant leg, "I gotta new dolly. Wanna see? Wanna see?"

He reached down to her and lifted her up to his waist, "Sure," he said with an affectionate smile.

"See," she said, as she proudly held up the Malibu Barbie close to her uncle's face, "She pretty ain't her?"

"Yes, sweetie, she is." He responded.

"You got some serious rest, Bro," Sean interjected, "You were out for days...Was startin' to worry a little...How's your coconut?"

"It doesn't hurt, but I still feel a little dizzy now and then." Steve replied.

"You'll be okay. The doctor said that was to be

expected." Katie said with surety.

Sean continued in his usual joking manner, "Detective Barton filled us in on what happened...Something about somebody using your head as a basketball, dude."

Katie tried not to laugh as Damon giggled loudly in his squeaky four-year-olds voice.

Steve tried not to laugh, but couldn't help letting out a small one, "Actually, it felt more like my head was a bowling ball crashing into the pins," he chuckled.

They all moved towards the kitchen as the three oldest children made their way to the backyard to play. Katie held Nathan in her arms as he quietly sucked on his bottle, not having a care in the world.

"We had the breakfast bar at Shoney's this morning. Sorry you missed it, Goober!" Sean apologized.

"We didn't wanna' wake you," Katie added.

Steve opened the refrigerator. Katie noticed an astonished look came across his face at the site of a fully stocked ice box.

"We went grocery shopping yesterday...Think it was down to some stale bread and some... ummm...well, actually, I couldn't tell what the other stuff was in there...some brown pudding looking crap with a crack down the middle as big as the Grand Canyon and some white, well...grey...chunky stuff with little dancing fungi on it." Sean descriptively informed him.

Steve had a serious look on his face as he reached for the orange juice carton then turned to Sean, "The grey stuff...that is some evidence I was studying in a rape case."

Sean looked stunned as Katie's mouth dropped open. She touched her lips with the tips of her fingers, "Oh God," Katie said, "Sean, go out to the trash can out back and get it. I threw it out. Oh God Steve, I'm so sorry. I didn't--"

Steve cut her panic off, "I was just kidding you all!" He chuckled as he threw a 'gotcha' look at them both.

They all laughed as Nathan just stared at them with that look two-year-olds have when they seem to just stare at you as if you are crazy, never missing a beat as he steadily sucked on his bottle.

After the silliness subsided, Steve spoke, "I've got a lead in this new case I need to check out today. I can't get a hold of my partner, so, Sean... You wanna go with me?"

"Hell Yeah!" Sean replied enthusiastically, without hesitation, "We goin' now?"

"Yeah. I just need to shower and change first."

"Cool. I'm ready." The excitement in Sean's voice was clear.

"Okay, relax. I'll be ready in about 20 minutes," Steve replied.

Sean couldn't resist, "It'll be like... Starsky and Hutch, or Crockett and Tubbs, or..." He paused for a second, "Like--"

Steve interrupted him, "Jake and the Fatman?"

Sean threw him a look of disapproval, and then burst out laughing again. Katie joined in the laughter as she said, "You two are too much."

Steve then went upstairs to get ready.

Pray For Death

~ 29 ~

Sheriff Cagle kissed his wife goodbye. She wished him luck as he left for the election polls. They opened at 10:00am and he wanted to be a little early. He thought making a presence might help to encourage the swing voters this year. He arrived at City Hall at about 8:45. The hallways were quiet. Only a security guard stood just inside the entrance. The Sheriff bypassed the metal detector as the guard greeted him. Buster didn't answer but nodded back instead. He made his way down a short hallway to a break room where he fixed himself a cup of coffee. His left hand was trembling as he tried to hold the Styrofoam cup in it. He focused on the cup for a moment as he steadied his hand from shaking. He then made his way over to a table in the center of the room and sat down. He picked up a remote in front of him and pointed it at the small television bracketed to the wall above him. He turned it on and flipped through the stations, stopping briefly to see who the guest was on Regis & Kelly... It was Russell Crowe. He continued to flip though the channels to the local news station. He settled in a chair as a Viagra commercial only added to his aging insecurities.

Pray For Death

~ 30 ~

Steve was ready to go about 30 minutes later. Sean had also changed his clothes to a pair of blue jeans and a long sleeve button down shirt. Steve came down the stairs without the bandage on his head and an extra bullet proof vest in his hand. He met Sean in the living room and tossed the vest at him, "No chances, Okay?" he said as he stared seriously at his brother.

"Yeah...okay... sure," Sean replied in a similar tone as he started to unbutton his shirt. Sean made his way around the house to kiss all the children goodbye. He then gave Katie a big hug and assured her that he would be careful. Katie didn't seem worried. She trusted Steve as a police officer and as a family member, and knew that he would do everything in his power to keep Sean safe. She acknowledged Sean's excitement with a smile and gave him a long kiss on the lips. Sean then joined Steve, who was already waiting in the vehicle. Once in the Explorer, Sean opened the conversation by asking where they were headed.

Steve informed him, with little detail about the conversation he had just had with Marcus.

"Cool...so you think this guy is the Slasher?" Sean

asked with enthusiasm.

"Don't know...could be...so we need to be cautious." He pointed at the glove box, "You'd better take that handgun again," he directed.

Sean opened the glove box and retrieved the pistol, once again checking the safety, then sliding it into his belt.

They arrived at the Mountain View Apartments about fifteen minutes later. Steve directed his brother to look for apartment #215. After circling around three different buildings, Sean pointed out his passenger window, "There it is, on the second floor." Steve parked in an empty space and shut off the vehicle. He took a deep breath and looked over at his brother, "All seriousness here, bro...okay?"

Sean nodded, "Yeah...got it." The two exited the vehicle and began walking towards the staircase.

"Put that thing in the back," Steve ordered his brother, as he pointed to the pistol in Sean's belt, "Gotta look professional." Sean immediately moved the gun from the front of his pants to the back as instructed.

Steve went up the exterior stairs. Sean followed

closely behind him, looking around in every direction, as they made their way to the second floor landing.

When they reached the top, Steve' pointed just past the door that read '215', and quietly told his brother to move to that position. Sean silently complied.

There was a blank, white envelope taped to the center of the door. Steve ignored it as he solidly knocked three times on the aluminum door. A few moments passed and no response. Steve knocked again. Still no answer. Sean pointed to the envelope as an indication that he thought Steve should retrieve it and look at its contents. Steve hesitated for a moment, looking down the outdoor hallway and back towards the parking lot, then took the envelope off of the door. It wasn't sealed. He proceeded to open it and pulled out a single white sheet of paper. He unfolded it and read the typed words on it to himself: 'Come in Detective Layton. It's about time you got here. Don't worry, I'm not here. But I think you'll find something interesting inside'.

After reading it, Detective Layton paused for a moment as he looked at his brother with a bewildered stare.

Sean returned the look with one of curiosity as he

silently mouthed the word "What?"

Steve handed his brother the note to read. As Sean read it to himself, Steve removed his 9mm pistol from his shoulder holster and clicked the safety switch to the 'Fire' position. When Sean looked up at him in amazement, Steve instructed him in a whisper to "Stay put". Sean nodded in compliance.

Detective Layton reached for the door handle, quietly turned it and slowly opened the door. Its hinges creaked for the first eight inches or so, and then stopped. Steve pushed the door fully open as he released the handle. Inside, it was dark and the pungent odor of bleach instantly hit Steve in the face, causing his eyes to water. He pulled a handkerchief form his back pocket and cupped it over his nose and mouth as he entered the apartment. He kept his pistol raised and pointed it around the room. He checked the light switch on the wall, but nothing happened. There was enough light coming through the windows for him to make his way around. He continued past the kitchen to a short hallway on the left. He wanted to make sure no one was in the apartment before looking at its contents.

As he entered the hallway he could clearly see

that no one was in the small bathroom to his left. In front of him was a shut door. It was the only other doorway in the apartment, so he presumed it led to the bedroom. He hesitated before opening it, as flashbacks of the crime scenes in this case alternated in his head. He began to breathe heavily through the handkerchief as sweat began streaming down his face. The sound of his own heartbeat beginning to get louder as it echoed inside of his head.

He counted to three and then slung the door open. He immediately pointed his pistol around the room. The light was coming in through a bare window to his right and illuminated the only thing visible in the room -- a bassinet.

The sound of a newborn infant baby crying in a tunnel was gradually getting louder and louder. Steve looked over at the open closet. It was empty. He then slowly walked towards the bassinet as the crying became almost unbearable. As he peered over the edge, he noticed a small life-sized infant doll in it. It was carefully wrapped in a blue baby blanket.

Steve holstered his weapon and carefully lifted the doll as if it were a real child. When he did, the crying immediately stopped. Steve seemed mesmerized by the lifelike doll. He stared at it for a few moments as time felt like it stopped. He then unwrapped the small blanket from around the doll. Underneath, the doll was wearing a small t-shirt with just two words on it -- 'Baby Layton'.

Steve immediately threw the doll down into the bassinet. The crying began again, but started off loudly this time, and began to fade as Steve took slow steps backwards towards the bedroom doorway, never taking his eyes off the bassinet, a distraught look on his face.

"Hey!" A voice squalled from behind him. Steve jumped as it startled him. He swung around while reaching for his gun. He realized it was his brother before his gun made it out of its holster.

"Geezis Fucking Christ, Sean...you scared the living hell out of me!"

"Sorry Steve...I just couldn't keep waiting outside. It looks like no one's here anyhow." Sean looked at his brother's face closely, "You okay bro? You look like shit. What's in here?"

Steve didn't turn towards the bassinet, but simply pointed over his shoulder with his thumb. Sean immediately brushed past him and walked over to the bassinet. He picked up the doll and read the t- shirt, "Holy shit, Steve. What the fuck is going on?" He turned to look at his brother, but he had left the room. Sean made his way to the living area where he found Steve knelt down in front of a telephone on the floor in the middle on the room. There was nothing else in the room. Steve was just sitting there with his chin in his right hand, staring at the phone. Sean asked him again if he was okay, but he didn't answer. As Sean looked closer, he noticed that his brother wasn't staring at the phone. He was staring at a telephone number that had been carved into the carpet.

"What the ---"

Steve cut him off, "Shhh."

There was silence for a few moments as neither man moved. Then Steve spoke, "I know this number," he said in a low tone, and then repeated it louder, "I fucking know this number!"

Sean asked.

Steve thought for a moment more, trying to recollect how this telephone number was familiar to him. He pulled out his cell phone and started scrolling through his phonebook entries. Sean just looked on, dazed and confused, as his brother almost seemed frantic while pressing buttons on his cell phone pad. Suddenly he stopped and stared into the LED screen, holding it up so he could see it and the number in the carpet at the same time.

"Summer...Sweet Jesus. It's fucking Summer's!" He suddenly blurted out.

"Who the hell is Summer?" Sean asked.

Steve didn't answer him. He was dialing Summer's number on his cell phone. He stood up and began pacing back and forth in the room as he listened and counted the rings out loud, "One...Two...Three."

There was a click, "Summer?" Steve uttered.

A man's voice answered, but was obviously a recording. The voice sounded digitally altered and said in a sinister tone, "One stripper, two stripper, sweet little pie...You better catch me quick...or Summer will die...Hello Steve, be sure to check the baby's diaper before you put him to bed." The recording ended with a long beep then a dial tone.

Steve hung up and frantically scurried back to the bedroom he picked up the doll and slid its diaper down.

As he did, a folded photograph fell out of it and onto the floor. He immediately knelt down and laid the doll on the floor next to him, as he picked up the photograph with his other hand. He could not have even imagined what he was about to see. On the back was written 'dqueen87'. He slowly unfolded the photo as his brother stared on silently from behind him. On the 5 x 8 glossy paper was the images of Debbie and his stillborn child on the night he found their lifeless bodies. A multitude of emotions came swarming over Steve, as his hands began to shake. Sorrow filled his face, while pain and anguish found its way to his stomach. His chest began to ache and tears formed in his eyes, as he knelt there silently staring at the graphic image. He suddenly stood up as the room began to slowly spin around him. Every emotion was suddenly replaced by pure rage. He crushed the photograph in his left hand as he raised both arms in the air and screamed, "I'll get you for this...I'll get you, you motherfucker!"

Pray For Death

~ 31 ~

It's like a friggen' Stephen King novel, Mom…Yeah…Susanna Moore…Yeah, I guess your right... more like Moore," Sean agreed as he shifted the telephone from one ear to the other, "He's fine. The doctor gave him a sedative…Yeah, we're all okay too. I'll call you back in a few days…Sure…Love you too…Bye." Sean hung up the phone. He had called his folks in Miami, to fill them in on the latest news. He had always had a better relationship with their parents than Steve had. His brother would have probably slit his own wrists before ever voluntarily sharing any current events with them. Steve didn't hate his parents. He just didn't believe that they actually gave a crap about him, or his life. He had moved out of his parent's home when he was just sixteen, and had moved in with his best friend, Ivan, and his mother. He had stayed with them until he graduated high school. Since then, he had had very little contact with his parents. Mostly just visits at Christmastime and the occasional phone call on birthdays and such.

Sean, on the other hand, had always brown- nosed his folks. Since his adult life had always been less stable than Steve's, he'd always made sure to 'butter his bread' on both sides. He had always needed his parents help, mostly financially, so he made sure to always keep them within arm's reach.

~ 32 ~

October 31st - was sleeping face down on a large bed covered in silver satin sheets. She was completely naked. Her hands and feet were tied to the four corner posts and a black satin blind fold covered her eyes. Several candles dimly lit the room. They flickered as a slight breeze stirred through the room.

The sinister sounds of Type O Negative's - 'Black No. 1' played loudly on a portable boom box sitting on a nearby dresser: 'I went on patrol...and boy, I found her...She's in love with herself...She likes the dark...On her milk white neck...the devil's mark...Now it's all Hallow's Eve...the moon is full...but will she trick or treat...I bet she will...She will . . .'

Summer suddenly awoke. She slowly lifted her head as far as she could and struggled with her restraints for a moment. Realizing that she couldn't get free, she stopped struggling and attempted to slide the blindfold up by dragging her head back and forth on the bed. Within moments, she managed to get it slid slightly above one eye. She twisted her head around in every direction, trying to see as much in the room as possible. She absorbed as much as she could. The room was small, with dark wooden walls. She couldn't see any windows, but the walls were covered with a vast array of stuffed and mounted fish. The room smelled surprisingly clean. It had a strong orange citrus smell. She looked at the restraint that was tied around one of her wrists. It seemed to be a telephone cord. She tugged on it slightly, but quit when she realized it was only making it tighten down harder on her wrist. She lay her head back down and tried not to cry. Within moments, she was asleep again.

~ 33 ~

By 9:30am, City Hall was packed full of voters – even more than Sheriff Cagle had expected. The lines to the polling booths were growing rapidly. Busters stood just inside the front hallway entrance, greeting what he hoped were his constituents. Most of them seemed receptive to his presence. Buster was trying hard to keep a smile on his face, but his worries were eating away at him. He had also fully expected to see his adversary, Joel Yager, at the polls, but he was nowhere in sight. Buster didn't know what to think of his absence, '*Was he so confident of winning that he didn't feel the need to come out to the polls? Or maybe, he was just running late?*' Buster was thinking to himself.

Just then, Detective Barton strolled in, "Good morning, Sheriff."

"Mornin'," Buster greeted back.

Barton could tell by the tone in the Sheriff's voice that he was nervous, "Don't worry boss," he attempted to console, "You'll win this thing."

The Sheriff just nodded his head and changed the subject, "How's Steve?" He asked.

Detective Barton shook his head from side to side and shrugged one shoulder, "Don't know. Haven't seen him since he got his skull cracked. Guess I should stop by and see though."

"I called a couple of days ago, but his sister-in-law said he was still laid up in the bed," the Sheriff replied, "Then he was off runnin' down a lead when I called this mornin'."

Barton looked confused, "He's workin' a lead without me?"

"Yup, his sister-in-law said he had tried to get a hold of you before he left, but said he couldn't." Buster replied.

Barton immediately reached for his cell phone in his coat pocket. It wasn't there. He checked some of his other pockets, but realized that he didn't have it at all.

"Well, that would be why," the Sheriff added smugly.

"I'll get a hold of him and get back to you later today, Sheriff," Barton replied in embarrassment.

"You do that," Buster replied gruffly.

"Yes sir...and good luck to you here."

Barton made his way to the front of the line where he flashed his badge at the security officer, who allowed him to go into a booth to cast his vote. Once inside, Barton punched a hole in the box next to 'Joel Yager'.

The differences on most issues between Buster Cagle and Joel Yager had not been real earth shattering. However, the biggest difference in their issues was regarding County Police Officer Salaries. Buster believed in cut backs and salary reductions – to cut spending, while Joel was pushing for dramatic increases. Joel's campaign motto had been 'Crime doesn't pay – And neither does Buncombe County!' If Joel won the election for Sheriff, and Clinton Devereux, the incumbent, won the County Commissioner election, they would be the most powerful team in Western North Carolina. Everyone knew both their campaigns had been funded mostly by the local Evangelist, Bobby Gravely.

Clinton Devereux was a native of North Carolina - born and raised in Charlotte. Although extremely intelligent, his selfishness had made him a lonely man, when it came to friends. He had attended Western

Carolina University and later gone on to Law School at Duke University School of Law. At just forty-three years of age, he had already accomplished more than most individuals do in a lifetime. In the fifteen years since receiving his law degree, he had climbed – or more accurately described – 'clawed' his way up the political ladder. He had already been a Vice Mayor, Mayor, City Councilman and the District Attorney. Now, he was running for County Commissioner and hoped in four years to run for State Governor.

He had been married for nine years now, which went against the grain of his personality. His love of power and prestige should have kept him a single man, with little time to handle a wife or family; however, he was well aware that wives were excellent leverage in the political arena. His looks, and enormous inheritance, had always caused the 'Socialite Gold-diggers' to swoon around him. He was 6'2" and 204 lbs. of solid muscle...which didn't hurt his appeal either. He was rich, handsome and successful. A triple combination that men would kill to have. He had settled for an average looking accountant to fill the 'wifey' roll.

~ 34 ~

Steve awoke feeling groggy. He tried to focus his eyesight on different things in his bedroom, but couldn't get the blur out of his vision.

"Sean!" he yelled, but realized it came out a bit garbled.

He cleared his throat and then yelled again, "Sean?"

He listened for a response, or the sound of footprints on the hardwood staircase, but there were none.

He decided to get out of bed and threw his legs over the side. When he realized his leather slippers were lined up neatly by the bed, he slid his feet into them and pushed himself up to his feet. A sudden rush of blood went to his head causing him to wobble for a moment. He caught his balance and again attempted to focus on his surroundings. This time, as he strained his eyes, his vision began to clear. He rubbed his eyes vigorously with both curled up hands, then re-opened them. He could now see quite clearly as he shuffled towards the bathroom. On his way, he briefly checked the time on his wristwatch. It read 2:36. He knew it had to be in the afternoon from the bright sunlight trailing through the window.

He reached the sink and turned on the water to regulate it to a lukewarm temperature, before splashing it on his face. He stared silently into the vanity mirror. His face looked pale and rough. Dark circles hung below his eyes and his beard had three to four days growth. He stroked his facial hair for a moment as he continued to stare at his own reflection. Suddenly, he felt water rising on the fingertips of his right hand that was holding the edge of the sink. He quickly glanced down into the porcelain sink and noticed the color of the water looked rusty. He looked next to the sink and noticed the rubber stopper was not in the hole. He shut off the water just before it overflowed. He looked around the bathroom for something he could use to unclog the drain, but couldn't find anything suitable. He bent over next to the toilet bowl and retrieved a plunger from the small cabinet. As he returned to the sink, he noticed the water had become much darker and now was more of a dark red color. He stuck the plunger into the sink and pumped it up and down a few times. The water immediately began to drain very quickly. He could barely make out something near the edge of the drain through the murky water. He reached in and picked up the item just as the last bit of swirling water exited the basin. He immediately knew it was a severed human finger.

All things considered, Detective Layton was hardly mortified – as he should have been. He was slightly shocked, but only showed a small grimace as he gently placed the finger on the counter next to the sink. He grabbed a hand towel from the bar next to him and dried his hands. He then went back into the bedroom and picked up the telephone receiver and dialed his partner's cell phone.

"Barton" a voice answered.

"Hey Ken, it's Steve--"

"Geezis Christ, Steve. It's about friggen' time you called. You alright?" Barton interrupted.

"Well...actually...no, I'm not."

"What the hell is it now?" Barton asked.

"I need you to come over."

"Now?"

"Yeah, right away," Steve instructed.

"Okay, sure. What is it?"

"Just get over here."

"Okay. I'm on my way now. I'll be there in a few minutes."

Steve hung up the receiver with his forefinger, then released it and dialed another number.

The number rang twice, "Hello," Marcus answered.

"It's me, Layton."

"Yeah, I know," Marcus replied matter-of-factly.

"I need your help."

"I don't know, man. This shit is freakin' me out. This psycho is off the charts--"

Detective Layton interrupted, "Marcus. I really need your help on this one now! He's got Summer. Well, I think he still does. I don't what day it is anymore."

"Summer? Summer Stevenson?" Marcus asked surprisingly.

"Goddamn, Marcus. Is there anyone you don't fucking know?" Steve exclaimed.

"I know everyone, man."

"So, how the hell do you know Summer? She's not a stripper," he paused for a moment, "or is she?"

"No, she ain't a stripper. She's just a college student at WCU, and she works part time at the Biltmore Estate."

Steve seemed puzzled by the information. '*How does she fit into all of this if she isn't a dancer?*' he asked himself, '*There's got to be a connection.*'

"Why the fuck would he kidnap her then?" he asked Marcus.

"I don't know, man. Maybe he ain't just goin' after strippers anymore," Marcus replied.

"Yeah, obviously. But, there's got to be a reason why he picked her. She was a witness to one of the crime scenes recently, you know." Steve informed.

"No, I didn't know that. But, how would this psycho know that?"

Steve thought for a moment about what Marcus just said, '*How would he know?*'

"You're right, Marcus. How could he have known? We didn't publicize her name in anything but the police report...and no one should have access to that except law enforcement personnel working on the case."

"I guess," Marcus replied, "so what do you need me for?"

"Oh yeah. I think the attacker left me a clue to his identity. On the back of a photograph, he wrote the word *dqueen87.*"

"dqueen87? Sounds like an internet screen name or something."

"Yeah, that's what I think too," Layton agreed.

"But why would he leave that? Isn't that easy to trace?" Marcus asked.

"Actually, it's not. First, you'd have to know what it's a screen name for. It could be for an ISP account, like AOL or Yahoo, or just for an individual website somewhere on the internet. Even if we pinpointed it, most likely the registered account info is bogus.

"Yeah, probably."

"We'd only be able to trace the account holder if he used a credit card to pay for the services. And even then, there could be a dqueen87 being used with all the major ISPs...and I'm sure with hundreds, or even thousands of individual websites out there, it would be an impossible task," Layton added.

"Hmmm? Well, maybe it's a chartroom screen name?"

"Chat room?"

"Yeah...You know what a chartroom is, don't you?" Marcus said sarcastically.

"Sure."

"It could be this crazy fucker's identity on the web. Most people use the same chat name at dozens of different sites. It's easier to remember your logins that way," Marcus explained.

"I didn't know that. But that goes to show how much I chat on the internet...Never! And that doesn't really help much, now, does it?... Being there are thousands and thousands of chat services. Right?"

"Yeah, there are thousands, but you could probably narrow that down a lot."

"How?" Steve asked.

"Well, you just start eliminating them."

"Eliminating them?"

"Dude, come on, Mr. Detective! Yeah, you know...based on things like geography, topics, etc," Marcus explained.

"Oh...I see...I don't know shit about these chat rooms.

"Obviously."

"Okay... then here... Why don't you help me search these chat rooms?"

"Me? Come on, man. I got better things to do than sit at the library and search chat rooms!" Marcus replied.

"The library? You don't have internet service at your house?"

"No."

"Oh," Layton thought for a moment, "Okay...how about this? I need to go out of town for a few days...so why don't you stay at my place while I am gone?"

"Your place?"

"Yeah, my place. I've got high speed cable internet."

"You want me to stay at your house and surf the internet while you're out of town?" Marcus asked in a surprised voice.

"Yeah, why not?"

"Ummm? Cuz' I wouldn't know what to do in a place that big."

"Big?" Layton asked, then realized he shouldn't be condescending, "Oh… you'll be fine."

"Ain't your brother and his family stayin' with you?" Marcus asked.

"Yeah, but they're leaving tomorrow."

"I don't know, man. I--"

Steve interrupted, "Marcus, just fucking do it!

What's the big deal? Just hang out at my place while I'm gone, and check out as many chat rooms as you can. Just try to find someone using that name… okay?"

Marcus didn't answer.

"Look… there's plenty of food and shit… you won't need anything while you're here. It's not gonna' kill you!"

"I really don't--"

"Marcus!" Steve yelled into the phone.

"Alright. Alright, man!" Marcus conceded.

"Come by day after tomorrow. I'll show you around and give you a key."

"Yeah."

"Alright, be cool." Steve said, trying to be hip.

"Huh?"

Layton hung up the phone and then sat down on the couch to collect his thoughts. He now knew that he had to treat everyone as a suspect. He couldn't exclude anyone from suspicion. Not even his partner or Agent

Raney. He felt as though he was losing his mind. He knew he was all alone, and that it was personal between this attacker and himself.

'*Attacker*?' he thought. He needed desperately now to give a name to this lunatic. Attacker just wouldn't cut it anymore. He stroked his chin for a few moments, and then blurted out, "Satin Psycho. Yeah, that's what you are you fucking bastard… The Satin Psycho!"

A few moments later, Detective Barton knocked on the front door.

Layton got up and opened the door.

"Damn, Steve… you look like shit," Barton said as he entered the house.

"Thanks, 'preciate that," Layton responded sarcastically.

Barton immediately made his way to the kitchen and opened the refrigerator. He stood there with the door open, surveying the shelves. When he spotted a can or Mountain Dew, he grabbed it and shut the door.

Layton had followed him into the kitchen and propped himself on a stool at the bar. Barton joined him as he opened the can of soda with his excessively large pocket knife. His unusual method of opening the can caught Layton's attention. Steve watched curiously as his partner slid the blade underneath the aluminum tab and rocked it upwards. Barton then folded the lock blade with one hand and slid it back into the rear pocket of his slacks.

"So, what did you need?" Barton asked nonchalantly.

Layton immediately raised one eyebrow and looked up at Barton's face. Layton still had the same look on his face, "I had a visitor recently," he replied.

"Yeah, who?" Barton asked nonchalantly, as he took a large gulp of soda.

"Our boy."

Barton looked puzzled, "Our boy?"

"Yup."

"Here? The guy was here?"

Layton raised both eyebrows and nodded his head, "Yeah, and he left one of his trophies in my bathroom."

"What?"

"I think it's Scarlet's ring finger."

"The third victim?"

"Yeah."

"Geezis Christ, Steve. Did you call it in?"

"No."

"No? Why the fuck not?"

"Cuz' I didn't want forensics tramping all over my house," Steve replied.

"But--"

Layton interrupted, "But nothing... I'm just gonna' bag it up myself. You know as well as I do that this shithead didn't leave anything behind. He's clean. He's always clean."

"Yeah, but procedure says--"

"Fuck Procedure!" Layton snapped. "This scumbag has made this whole fucking thing personal. I don't give a shit about fucking procedure right now."

"Alright. Okay. Relax, Steve."

"I want you to bring it downtown for me, Ken."

"Okay, sure. But what do I tell them?"

"I don't give a rat's ass what you tell them. Just tell them it was found in my house."

"That's gonna' be kinda' difficult to pass off without suspicion," Barton told him.

"You'll think of something."

"Alright… then what?" Barton asked.

Layton thought about what he could have Barton do next. He didn't want him to be hanging out with him while he looked for Summer, so he needed to have him do something that would keep him occupied for at least a few days.

Suddenly, a thought came to his mind, "What have you been working on for the last few days or so?" he asked.

Detective Barton seemed unprepared to answer the question. He stuttered a little as he answered, "Well, ummm… actually… well… nothing on this case. The

Sheriff gave me another old homicide case to reopen."

Layton was surprised to hear this, but tried not to show it, "Okay… work on that, and I'll get back to you in a few days on this case. I'm just gonna' retrace our steps in this investigation up until now, to see if we've missed anything," he lied.

Detective Barton was completely caught off guard by Layton's response and asked almost disappointedly, "You're not going to look for Summer?"

Oddly enough, that was just the response Layton had expected to hear, but again, he was considering everyone a suspect now. He wasn't going to open up his game book for the defense to read, "I got a lot to cover. Missing Persons is already on the case. Of course I will keep my eyes and ears open for any leads to her whereabouts though. I highly doubt she is still alive, though. It's been days now," Layton responded without allowing Barton to know that he really did believe that Summer was still alive.

Barton didn't quite seem to know how to respond to that, but didn't make a big stink of it as he knew that Detective Layton hadn't been himself lately - for good reason. He just nodded his head and agreed to call Layton in a few days. He then asked Layton to retrieve the finger for him, so he could be on his way.

"Yeah, right...the finger... Oh, by the way... where is Agent Raney? I thought he'd be with you." He asked.

"Oh, Yeah... He went back to Raleigh. Said he had some vacation time he had to use, or he would lose it. Told me to have you call him next week if you needed him to come back then."

The more information Layton got about everything surrounding this case, the more confused he felt. Nothing seemed to make sense. He shook his head back and forth and made his way over to a cabinet drawer. There he retrieved a Ziploc sandwich baggie and filled it half way with ice. He handed it to Detective Barton and told him he could retrieve the finger from next to his bathroom sink upstairs.

Barton took the baggie from him and immediately headed upstairs, while Layton put on a pot of coffee.

A few moments later Barton returned holding the plastic sandwich bag, "Alright, I'm outta here... and Steve... be careful... will ya?"

"Yeah... I will," Steve replied.

"Call me in a few days and bring me up to speed... okay?"

"Sure," Layton responded with an upward twitch of his head.

Detective Barton gave Layton half wave then left.

Layton poured himself a cup of coffee then retreated to his den. He logged into his computer and proceeded to set up an internet user account for Marcus. As he did so, he remembered his original deal with Marcus and realized that he hadn't contacted his friend at the department of social services. He picked up the phone on the desk as he flipped through his Rolodex. He found the number and dialed his friend Annette Richards.

~~~~~~~~~

Annette had been Debbie's best friend for years. They had also worked closely on many legal cases, mostly ones involving children. Steve had always had a feeling that Annette had liked him more than just a friend. She had always seemed overly and obviously flirtatious.
~~~~~~~~~

This had always made Steve uncomfortable because she was so attractive. He used to be worried that Debbie would see Annette's actions as threatening, but she never seemed to. He figured Debbie wasn't oblivious to the passes Annette made, but for some unknown reason, she had tolerated it. Steve had always assumed it was just Debbie's confidence in their relationship.

A sweet, sexy southern voice answered the phone, "Annette Richards, can I help you?"

Steve hesitated for a moment as the hair stood up on the back of his neck. It always did when he heard her voice.

She broke the silence, "Hello?"

"Annette... hey," Steve cleared his throat, "It's Steve... Steve Layton."

"Steve, oh my gawd"... How the hell are you?"

"Good, Annette... how about you?"

"I'm doin' just fine darling... I can't believe it's you... what has it been?... like two or three years... right?"

Steve almost melted at her voice. *'God it was unbelievably sexy'*, he thought.

"Yeah, it's been a while… Sorry I haven't kept in touch lately… but you know."

"Don't worry about it Steve… I understand."

"You always were understanding, Annette… Thanks."

Annette blushed a little on the other end of the line. She could feel a tingle running down her spine and goose bumps on her legs. She had more than just had an infatuation with Steve years ago… She was truly in love with him. Many times over the years she had wanted to tell him, but swore that she would never do that to her best friend. Then, after Debbie died, she had tried on several occasions, including at her funeral, to let Steve know how she really felt. Steve had been such an emotional wreck the first year after her death, that he barely even noticed her increased advances. Hell, he had even been put on administrative leave by the department for the first nine months. When he had returned to work, he had buried himself so deep in his work that he didn't have the time or the emotions to share with anyone - let alone a female companion.

"So what do I owe the pleasure of this call to?"

"Actually… I need professional favor Annette."

Annette pouted playfully, "Okay Steve, what do you need?"

"I have a friend, well sort of a friend… Anyhow, he's in a custody battle over his daughter. His ex keeps filing bogus reports with you guys, so she has some ammunition against him in court," Steve began explaining.

"Bogus?... How do you know the reports aren't valid?"

"Trust me, Annette. I know this guy. The reports are bullshit," Steve said slightly irritated.

"Okay… so how can I help?"

"Well, it seems that whoever has been assigned to this case is either an idiot, or is in the mother's pocket. I'm just asking if you could look into it personally… since you are a supervisor there."

"Of course, Steve, anything for you… but I can't guarantee anything okay?"

"I know."

"So what's your friend's name?" Annette asked.

"Marcus Starr," He spelled it out, "S-T-A-R-R"

"Alright, I'll check into it… but there's one catch." Annette added with a sneaky smile.

"Catch?" Steve replied puzzledly.

"Yes, darling… you have to have dinner with me to get the results."

Steve knew that Annette was dead serious. He was about to object politely, then realized it wouldn't be such a bad thing to have dinner with her.

"Okay, call me when you know something," Steve responded as he pictured Annette's 5'5" blonde frame in a sexy, white, low-cut dinner dress.

"Bye Steve."

"Bye Annette." Steve returned to his initial task setting up the internet account. He came up with a creative username to add to his internet account he typed in '1badhustler', and then completed the couple more steps to set up the account.

When he finished, he logged off of the master

screen name and went upstairs to shower and pack a travel bag. He stood in front of the vanity mirror naked, brushing his teeth. The thought of undressing Annette slowly, and making love to her, started going thought his mind. He could feel his penis begin to throb lightly as it hardened. By the time he finished brushing and rinsed out his mouth, he had a full stiff erection.

He stepped into the already steaming shower and closed the glass door behind him. He stood under the pelting stream of hot water and stroked himself slowly, as he envisioned himself sliding in and out of Annette. He actually knew exactly what she looked like naked. A friend of his had informed him years and that Annette had posed for a College Girls Edition of Playboy when she was 21. at first he hadn't wanted to see her layout in the magazine, but a year or so later his curiosity had gotten the best of him while having a few beers at a friend's house. Of course he never mentioned to Annette, or Debbie, that he ever had any knowledge of the provocative spread.

Steve continued imagining himself having erotic sex with Annette, until he had an orgasm. His knees felt so weak he almost fell to the shower floor. He steadied himself with a tight grip on the brass washcloth bar, as he changed the water to a cooler temperature. A few moments later he regained his strength and stepped out of the shower. He dried himself off and stared at his new facial hair in the mirror. It wasn't long, just about a week's growth. He stroked his fingers over it approvingly and gave himself a wink.

Pray For Death

~ 35 ~

Betty Joe arrived at City Hall around 6:30pm. She strolled through the metal detector as the usual swarm of heads turned to stare at her ageless beauty. She wore her traditionally glamorous smile and returned every greeting with a sassy southern 'Good evenin'. She carried a foil wrapped plate of food in her left hand as she made her way down the hallway to break room where Buster was nervously pacing back and forth.

At the mere site of her entering the room, Buster's anxiety subsided. Suddenly he felt at ease, as she gave him a loving hug and kiss.

"Did you cast your vote yet?" Buster asked.

"No, not yet… I'm headed down there now."

"You don't have much time," Buster replied with a sense of urgency.

"I'm goin' sweetheart… I'm goin." Betty Joe unwrapped the plate of food on the table and put it in the microwave. She set the timer and told her husband that he'd better have cleared the plate by the time she returned. Buster started to mumble something about not being hungry, but she quickly silenced him with a finger to his lips and a dominant glare. She then left the room and headed down the hallway to the voting booths. She had a bout twenty minutes before the polls closed, so her stride was brisk. As she passed back by the front doors, Detective Layton arrived. They greeted each other with a kiss on the cheeks and Betty Joe commented on liking his facial scruff. As Steve searched for a compliment to throw back at her, he couldn't help but notice her nipples standing erect underneath her dress. He immediately turned his eyes away and decided on a generic, "You look beautiful, as usual."

Betty Joe thanked him as they both continued down the hall.

After waiting in a short line, they both cast their votes for Buster. Betty Joe then made her way back down the hallway to the break room, while Detective Layton quickly left for the Police Station.

He arrived at the station about 7:30pm. There were limited personnel wandering the halls, mostly uniformed officers. Layton quickly made his way to his desk and removed several files from a bottom drawer. He briefly opened each to make sure he had the correct ones, and then picked up the telephone to dial home.

"Hello?" Sean answered.

"Hey Bro… What's up?"

"Not much… Katie's packing, the kids are watching Jurassic Park and I'm just straightening up… Didn't want to leave you a dirty house."

"I'll be there in about an hour or so."

"No prob… Katie cooked some Sheppard's Pie earlier. You can heat up a plate if you're hungry." Sean informed him.

"Thanks. I'm just reviewing some files at the station. I'm gonna' make one stop on the way home... so I'll be there soon."

"Okay… later," Sean replied.

"Later."

Steve hung up the phone, gathered up the files, then left.

About twenty minutes later he arrived at Charli's house. Anxiety overwhelmed him as he sat in the driveway staring at the front door, just as he had the other evening. He sat there for a while with a small gift wrap bag in his hand. In it was the perfume he had bought Charli for her birthday. He was trying to think of what to say to her, but he couldn't stop thinking about how he had been just minutes late the other night, 'If I had only been on time', he kept reciting in his head. His thoughts were now flashing back to the night he had found his wife and how he had been late that night too. The comparison seemed eerie and ironic. Now though; instead of envisioning his wife and child alone at the time of their demise; the thought was filled with a shadowy figure lurking around the room, waiting for Debbie to die, and then snapping that horrific photo.

Steve's daydreams were suddenly interrupted by a blinding flash of lightning, followed by large drops of rain pelting the windshield. He quickly grabbed his keys from the ignition and opened his car door. He got out and made a dash for Charli's front door, just as the thunder boomed.

The rain was frigid and his breath looked more like smoke than mist. He stood on the porch for a moment, shaking off the rain water, and then knocked gently. After no reply, he checked the door handle.

Surprisingly, it was unlocked. He cracked the door and called out for Charli, making sure to identify himself.

A voice called back softly from the living room, "Come in Steve."

He entered the house, removed his coat and hung it on a hook next to the door. The house was dark other than the flicker of glowing light from the fireplace. He walked towards the backside of the sofa in the center of the living room. As he made his way around it he could see Charli lying on it. She was propped up at one end reading a wedding magazine. A thick cotton blanket covered her body from her feet to her chest. Steve sat down near her feet. As the flames from the fireplace glowed on her face, he could see a tear streaming down her cheek.

Steve didn't know what to say. He had rehearsed it a couple of dozen times, but now that he was there, he just felt a large lump in his throat, and could find nothing more to say than, "I'm sorry."

"Don't be... it's not your fault," Charli replied softly, as she reached out and placed her hand on his.

~~~~~~~~~

Steve awoke to find himself lying next to Charli on the couch. The fireplace had been reduced to a few red embers, leaving the room chilled. He sat up and looked at his watch -- 3:00am. "Shit," he said in a whisper, trying not to wake Charli. He stood up and tucked the blanket around her, then added a couple of logs to the fire. He blew on the embers until a flame arose, and then slipped on his shoes. He gently brushed the hair away from Charli's face, kissed her gently on the forehead, then left, making sure to lock the front door from the inside before shutting it.

The wind had picked up and now howled through the large, bare oak trees surrounding the house. He flipped up the collar on his coat and hustled to his vehicle. The rain had stopped, but the full moon's light showed evidence of storm clouds still hovering overhead. He started his Explorer and turned the heat to full blast. While he waited for it to kick in, he searched his CDs for something to fit his mood. He put in Skid Row and skipped to '*I Remember You*'. As the song began, he passionately sang along... "*Woke up to the soothing sound of pouring rain... Wind will whisper and I think of you... All the tears you cried, they called my name... and when you needed me, I came through.*" He put the car in gear and drove for home.
~~~~~~~~~

~ 36 ~

7:00am was like a sledgehammer coming down on Steve's forehead. Between four children running up and down the stairs, and his brother singing '*Da Camp Town Ladies*' at the top of his lungs, he thought his nerves were going to bust out of his skin. He lay there with his eyes closed for a moment. His brother stopped singing momentarily as his bedroom door swung open. Sean stood there with a straw cowboy hat on and a small toy Sheriff's star pinned on his shirt. As Steve began to sit up, his brother began singing again as he slowly strolled into the room, "*He rode a blazing saddle... He wore a shining star... His job to offer battle, to bad men near and far...*" His brother slowly moved around the room as if he was in a Broadway musical, "*He conquered fear and he conquered hate... He turned our night in to day... He made his blazing saddle... A torch to light the way...*" Steve chuckled under his breath, grinned and shook his head back and forth, as he watched and listened to his brother's antics. Sean continued to sing as he approached the bed, "*When outlaws ruled the West, and fear filled the land... A cry went up for a man with guts... to take the West in hand... They needed a Man who was brave and true... with justice for all, as his aim... Then out of the sun, rode a man with a gun... and, Steve, was his name... Yes, Steve was his name.*"

Steve couldn't help but to laugh out loud now, as

Katie stood behind Sean giggling loudly, "You're such an idiot Goober!" he said jokingly, as he continued to shake his head back and forth.

Steve needed that laugh. He was about to be alone again, and this case had intensified his emotions to the point of exhaustion.

Katie handed him a cup of steaming coffee and a chocolate covered doughnut.

"Thanks. What time do you have to be at the airport?" Steve asked them.

"Around ten," Sean replied.

"Yeah, the plane leaves at eleven-fifteen," Katie added.

"Okay. I'll get up and ready."

"Thanks for letting us come, Goober," Sean said, as he removed the cowboy hat and placed it endearingly over his chest, "We needed this vacation!"

"Sure. No problem. Any time guys... You know that," Steve replied.

"I hope we cleaned up enough," Katie said with

an unsure look on her face.

"Yeah. It's great."

"Alright... we'll be downstairs," Sean added, ushering Katie out of the room.

Steve rolled out of bed and headed for the shower.

Ten minutes later he came down the stairs and joined his brother and Katie in the living room. They were watching 'A Few Good Men' on the big screen television, as Sean recited every word, without missing any of the actors' lines. After listening to Sean recite the entire courtroom scene between Tom Cruise and Jack Nicholson, Steve looked at his brother and chuckled. He sat down in his leather recliner and watched the rest of the movie with them.

Pray For Death

~ 37 ~

Marcus beat on the alarm clock a few times until the annoying buzzing stopped. He opened his eyes and took a quick glance at the time – 10:04am. He didn't have to be up early for anything in specific, but he wanted to check out a couple of things before he headed over to Detective Layton's place. He jumped out of bed and slid on a pair of Hilfiger jeans, a long sleeve Henley and his fine Italian leather shoes. He grabbed his car keys and jetted out the door in his usual hurried manner. He started the car and lit up the tires, leaving two long tracks on the cold pavement.

Ten minutes later he arrived at Diamonds, just as the owner was unlocking the front door. He jumped out of his vehicle and hollered at him, "Dean!"

"Hey Marcus... What's going on?"

The two shook hands.

"Not much man... just wondering if I could talk to you for a minute." Marcus asked.

"Sure thing," Dean replied, as he ushered Marcus into the dark club, "Let me turn on some lights."

Dean made his way over to a wall lined with a dozen switches. He selectively turned on four of them, and then called Marcus over to the bar. Marcus took a seat in one of the bar stools as Dean began setting up for the day's business.

"What can I do for you Marcus?"

Marcus hesitated for a moment before responding, "Dean... how long have we known each other? Ten years?"

Dean looked up from his task and stared Marcus straight in the eyes. He knew by Marcus's tone, that he had something serious on his mind, "Yeah... something like that... Why?""

"You wouldn't lie to me... would you?"

Dean looked a bit confused as he filled a small bin with fruit garnishes, "No, of course not. I wouldn't have any reason to. Why? What's up Marcus?"

"Rumor on the street is that Summer Stevenson is your daughter... Is that true?" Marcus responded.

Dean tried not to ask surprised by the question as he put a jar of cherries back into a small refrigerator underneath the bar, "Where did you hear that?"

"I'll take that as a yes, then... Geezis Dean--"

Dean interrupted him, "Look Marcus... I've got two P.I.'s working round the clock to find her... it's more than the fucking cops are doing!"

"You'd be surprised, man... I think they are actually bustin' a little ass on this one," Marcus responded assuringly.

"You think?"

"Let's just say, I've heard a few things."

Dean's tone changed to a solemn desperation, "I don't understand it though... Summer has never danced... why the fuck did this psycho snatch her?"

Marcus just shook his head, acknowledging that he had no idea either.

"There's got to be a reason... Maybe it's just because you own this place."

Dean leaned back against a beer cooler and hid his face in his hands, then dropped them both to the edge of the cooler, "She's my only daughter... my only child...

my baby girl," he whimpered.

Marcus sympathized with him, but didn't allow Dean's whimpering to change his demeanor. He remained firm in his questioning, "I've known Summer for years, man... How come she never mentioned you were her father?"

Dean composed himself the best that he could, "She hates me... this place... everything to do with this life. She didn't ever want anyone to know I was her father. That's why she went to live with her mother after the divorce. We've hardly spoken since then."

"How long ago was that?" Marcus asked.

"Eight years."

"Who's her momma?" Marcus asked.

Dean looked surprised and confused as to why Marcus asked this question. However, he answered it with little hesitation, "Nicole Ashton... well it's Devereux now... Nicole Devereux."

Marcus couldn't believe his ears. His jaw would have hit the floor if he hadn't grabbed his chin, "Clinton Devereux's wife?"

"Yup... that's her," Dean replied as he popped the top of a Budweiser bottle and took a large swallow.

Marcus's brain was turning so fast he couldn't even keep up with it. All of a sudden his thoughts felt like a huge jigsaw puzzle. All the information was there. Now, he just needed to unscramble it and slide the pieces together. However, he knew there were still some major pieces missing and wasn't sure if he would be able to make sense of it all.

After his momentary daze, he looked up at Dean and excused himself, then quickly headed for the door.

Dean hollered after him, "What's your interest in all of this?"

Marcus was too engulfed in thought to even hear him. He quickly exited the building, got in his car and sped off. He had one more stop he wanted to make before heading over to Detective Layton's place.

Pray For Death

~ 38 ~

Detective Layton stared down the long hallway as he reached for the door handle of room 215. The hospital seemed darker than usual, with only a dim light coming from the nurses' station. No one was in sight. He pulled down the door handle and slowly entered the room. The moonlight shown through the window giving just enough light to silhouette the items in the room. Layton pulled out a small flashlight and clicked it on. The beam of light was bright for only a split second before turning a dull golden yellow. It flickered a couple of times as he made his way towards the bed. Then, just as he reached the bed and lifted the light towards the head of it, the light failed. Layton tapped it a few times, but it did not respond. He whispered, "Summer... Summer, it's Steve." There was no answer. The muffled sounds of the raging snow storm outside were all he could hear. The whistling and howling almost seemed rhythmic, like an eerie song – the banging shutter outside the window set the tempo. Suddenly the window burst open and the snow and howling wind filled the room. Layton quickly made his way around the bed and tried to shut it, but it seemed the harder he pushed, the stronger the wind got. He kept pushing on the window until he finally got it shut. He locked it and stood there silently for a moment to catch his breath. He then made his way over to the bed again. The room was silent again except for the beeping sound of the EKG machine next to the bed. It was getting steadily louder and louder as Layton stood over the bed. He pulled out his Zippo lighter and fired it up. The golden orange glow filled the room. He could now see Summer apparently sleeping in the bed. Her body was draped from the breasts down, in a silvery satin sheet. He softly called out her name a couple of times as he nudged her arm. She didn't stir. He then reached for the top edge of the sheet and slowly slid it down, exposing her bare breasts, as the EKG monitor's beeping became almost ear piercing. He continued to slowly slide the sheet down her body. When he almost reached her waist he threw the sheet towards the foot of the bed, expecting to expose the rest of her body. There was none. She had been cut in two and her insides oozed out of her top half. Immediately the EKG beeping went to a solid tone, indicating she was dead.

~~~~~~~~

Layton began to yell as he sat up in his bed. His alarm clock was ringing a solid steady tone as the sweat poured from his body. It was only a brief moment before he realized it was only a bad dream.

He shut off the alarm clock and glanced out the window. The wind started to howl as a snow storm began. He looked over at the alarm clock – 11:30am. "Shit!" he said as he jumped up and realized he had wanted to
~~~~~~~~

awaken two hours earlier. He raced to the shower.

Pray For Death

~ 39 ~

The pounding on the door was thunderous. Layton slid his pistol into its holster and exited the bedroom. His voice was filled with agitation as he trotted down the stairs yelling, "Just a minute!"

He swung open the door to see Marcus standing there with a huge grin on his face, and a large black duffel bag strapped over his shoulder.

Layton didn't have to speak his disapproval of the neanderthalish way Marcus had been knocking – It was evident by the expression on his face.

"Just thought I would knock the way you cops love to," Marcus sneered.

Layton just side-cocked a grin and rolled his eyes as he stepped out of Marcus's way. "I didn't get a chance to make you a key, so I'm just gonna' leave you mine." He took the key off of his key ring and laid it in Marcus's hand, "Let me show you around."

~~~~~~~~~
~~~~~~~~~

The police station was so quiet you could have heard a snake slithering across the floor. Somber faces stared at each other, but no one dared to speak. Buster Cagle was no longer the Sheriff of Buncombe County. He had lost the election by a narrow margin, but not narrow enough to warrant a recount. As he slowly packed his personal belongings, he could only think of one thing. He picked up a picture of himself standing next to his beautiful wife. As his bottom lip quivered, he murmured, "I'm sorry I let you down."

~ 40 ~

Detective Layton needed to work without interruption or interference. This case had pushed him into a corner that no cop ever wanted to be pushed into. He was now alone, unable to trust anyone – even his own partner. Catching this maniac would be even harder now, and he knew it. But now he had a new motivation, a new desire to see that this psycho paid dearly. He had no intention of ever arresting him. He would find him, look him dead in the eyes... and kill him. There would be no protocol, no leniency, and no mercy. Whoever this blade wielding lunatic was, he would meet his maker at Steve's hands.

Steve drove a few miles up the Blue Ridge Parkway until he reached a clearing. He parked and stood on the small rock wall that acted as a guardrail. He looked out over the Great Smokey Mountains in the distance, and into the deep valley below. He raised one foot up onto the wall, as if he was a king surveying his kingdom. He had to try to make sense of all this. He had to focus on the case, but the more he tried, the more difficult it was. His mind only flashed scenes from his life with Debbie. He remembered first meeting her. It was 1988 - a Campus Life field trip in their Senior year of high school. They had ended up sitting next to each other on the fifteen hour trip from Miami to Gatlinburg, Tennessee. At first, he had found it difficult to speak to her. She was the most beautiful woman he had ever laid eyes on. Within an hour, though, she had looked over at him and smiled. 'Say something, Damnit... at least say hello' he had thought, but his chest and throat had immediately tightened up. He managed only an awkward grin and a nod. It would be hours later before they would be engulfed in laughter and conversation.

His mind slipped forward five months – The helicopter landed in the parking lot adjacent to the Hyatt Regency Hotel in downtown Miami. The rotors stopped and Debbie stepped out in a royal blue and white prom gown her mother had made for her. She was absolutely stunning. Steve stepped out next in his white tails. His bow tie and cummerbund matched Debbie's dress. A crowd had gathered in front of the hotel. Their astonishment was obvious as they had watched the helicopter land, and this stunning couple emerge.

He remembered Debbie crying as he hugged her tightly and kissed her goodbye from the tarmac and boarded the plane to the Persian Gulf - returning nine months later with an engagement ring in hand. This time, her tears were tears of joy, as she threw her arms around his neck and said, "Yes, I love you so much, Steve... Yes, yes, yes!"

He remembered sliding his arm around her shoulder as they stood there in the rain watching Debbie's parents being lowered into the ground.

His thoughts turned to making love to Debbie. Passion had always been his trademark. If they weren't making love on a moonlit beach somewhere, there would always be rose pedals or chocolate kisses surrounding them while they made love.

His last thought was gently caressing Debbie's stomach before leaving for work on that fateful day. He had placed his hand gently on her cheek as he softly kissed her lips goodbye for the last time.

Steve had been smiling throughout the memories, until the last one. A tear now streamed down his face and his smile had turned to a frown. He took a deep breath and exhaled slowly. He forced himself to change his thoughts. He began to focus on the details of the case.

He focused on the voice on the phone saying, *"One stripper... two strippers... sweet potato pie..."* Was *this a clue? Or just creative poetry? 'Why would Summer Die?' he thought, 'This isn't his MO. Why had it become a game? Why did this guy kill his wife and child years earlier? What's the connection? Who is this motherfucker? Is this case tied to the ones in Florida? Where the hell is Agent Raney? Why had he taken a vacation in the middle of all of this? Can Detective Barton be trusted? Wasn't that a strange way to open a can of soda? How does Marcus know so many goddamn people involved in this case? What was dqueen87?'*

"Think, goddamnit, Steve. Think," he murmured out loud.

He reached down and unclipped his cell phone from his belt. He dialed Agent Raney's number. It didn't ring, but went straight to voicemail, "This is Raney... You know what to do, so do it."

'That's an odd message,' Steve thought. After the beep, Steve left a message, "Agent Raney. This is Detective Layton in Asheville. I've got some questions for you. Call me back A.S.A.P., please, thanks."

He hung up and dialed Marcus.

"Yeah?" Marcus answered.

"Everything okay?" Steve asked.

"Yeah, why wouldn't it be?"

"Just checking. Any leads on the *dqueen87* thing?"

"No."

"Okay. Just let me know if anything comes up."

"Sure."

Steve hung up and tapped his chin with the cell phone a few times while he thought what to do next.

A few minutes later he dialed a number.

"Hello," Betty Joe answered.

"Hey Betty Joe, it's Steve. How are you?"

"Good, Steve. And you?" she replied.

"I'm okay. How's the Sherri–", he caught himself mid-word, "How's Buster?"

"He's been down in the basement all day... locked the door and won't answer."

"You think he's alright?" Steve asked.

"I can hear him fiddling around with stuff down there, so I assume he's fine."

"He's probably just sulking a bit, Betty Joe. I'm sure he'll be fine... probably just needs some time."

"You're probably right, Steve. He's a tough ole' bird, isn't he?"

"He sure is," Steve agreed, "I'll be outta town for a few days. If you need me, just holler."

"I'll do that, Steve, thanks."

"Take care, Betty Joe."

"You too, Steve."

"Bye."

"Bye."

Just as Betty Joe hung up the phone, a gunshot rang out through the basement. Although startled at first, she immediately knew what had happened. She began to sob as she fell against the kitchen wall and slid to the floor.

~ 41 ~

Goddamnit! Where the hell is Detective Layton?" The new Sheriff yelled across the squad room, "It's been two goddamn days and no one knows where my own Detectives are!"

Everyone in the room froze and looked over at Joel Yager. Some cringed. Some rolled their eyes without letting him see, but no one answered.

"Oh, I see how it's gonna be. I got a bunch of diehard loyalists on my fuckin' hands! Well, let me make something very clear. Cagle is yesterday's newspaper..." Joel Yager continued in a stern voice, "and just like yesterday's paper, he's permanently gone... thrown out with the rest of the goddamn trash. And let me tell you something, the county trash pile is huge... so there's plenty of room for anyone else who wants to join him there! So let's get on thing straight, there's a new Sheriff in town... and you're lookin' at him! Things are gonna' change drastically around here... and fast. I wasn't elected to be your friend. I was elected to clean up the goddamn mess in this county. To do what Cagle couldn't do for twenty years... keep this county safe... especially from this *goddamn*lunatic roaming the streets. They may be strippers, but they're strippers in *my*county. That makes it my problem now, and I won't stand for this bullshit in my county!"

A cowboy voice sounded out from the back of the room, "We're with you, Wyatt Earp. Let's gun the son of a bitch down at the OK Corral!"

The room broke into laughter, but abruptly stopped as soon as Yager opened his mouth again, "Who said that? Who *the fuck*said that?" He raged, "Step forward and show yourself! Who the fuck has the goddamn nerve to talk to me like that?"

A figure from the back of the room began to move forward through the small crowd. He was wearing a long black duster, black boots and a black cowboy hat tilted down on his face. As he reached the front of the crowd he kept his head tilted down and flipped the right side of his coat back from his hip, as if to expose a Colt loaded holster. Only a police badge and a cell phone were present though – clipped securely to his belt. The stranger hovered his right hand a few inches over the cell phone as he twitched his fingers rapidly back and forth, as if preparing to draw a weapon in a dual.

The room remained silent. Joel Yager stood still, quizzically staring as the intimidating figure.

The stranger spoke again as he slowly raised his head to expose his face, "I'm you're Huckleberry."

Pray For Death

~ **42** ~

Marcus bitched and moaned as he searched for hours through chat rooms all over the internet. So far, he had had no luck. He spun around in the large leather office chair and began to look at the photos hanging on Detective Layton's den walls. He needed a break from the computer, so he grabbed a photo album from one of the shelves. He began flipping through it until one picture seemed to stand out. It was a picture of a teenage boy standing next to a beautiful teenaged blonde, in what looked like a sub shop. Marcus removed the photo from the album and studied it closer. He realized that it was not a sub shop, but an ice cream shop. He assumed the teenage boy in the photo was Detective Layton, but didn't recognize the girl. He flipped it over. The date on the back read -- 06/1987. It also had a notation handwritten on it, Lindsey and Me. All of a sudden Marcus realized what dqueen87 was. It was short for 'Dairy Queen 1987'. He grabbed his cell phone and immediately called Detective Layton.

~~~~~~~~~

The stranger in black was Sean Layton. He pulled the cell phone from his belt and flipped it open. With his speed dial he made a call, while he held the phone
~~~~~~~~~

extended out to Joel Yager. The speaker phone came on as the phone dialed. Joel Yager hesitated, at first, before reaching slowly for the phone. As he took it from Sean's hand, a voice answered, "This is Steve Layton. I am hereby resigning my duties as a law enforcement officer with the Buncombe County Sheriff's Office, effective immediately. Here's my badge..." Sean unclipped the badge from his belt and handed it to Yager while Steve continued to speak, "My service pistol can be retrieved from my locker at the station. No further information is needed as to my whereabouts. Good day, gentlemen." The phone went silent as Sean held out his hand to retrieve it from Yager, who was standing there in awe. Sean held the cell phone out, as if it were a pistol, as he backed through the crowd, pointing it in different directions, until he disappeared through the doorway.

~~~~~~~~

Because Steve was on the phone with Joel Yager, Marcus had reached his voicemail. He left a brief message, "Detective Layton... It's Marcus... Call me back ASAP... It's important."   He hung up the phone and continued to search the internet, although he was sure he wouldn't find anything. He was positive he had already stumbled onto the attacker's identity.
~~~~~~~~

~~~~~~~~~

Sean had left his wife and children at the airport after Steve had dropped them all off. He had hugged and kissed them as if he was a Soldier going off to war. Katie objected, at first, but she had been married to Sean long enough to know that once he made up his mind to do something, there was no stopping him. She had made him promise to always wear a bullet proof vest, and to try not to be a hero.

Sean knew that he had to help his brother. He knew this case was either going to drive Steve mad, or kill him.

He had called Steve and taken a cab to meet up with him on the Blue Ridge Parkway. Steve had also vehemently objected to Sean's participation, but conceded when Sean showed up on the Mountain wearing the Black Duster and cowboy hat. He gave him a bulletproof vest and one of his backup pistols, once again reminding him of the seriousness of the situation.

Steve had waited in the parking lot across the street from the Police Station while Sean had returned the badge to Joel Yager. He had thought long and hard about his decision to quit the force. He knew he had to, in order to successfully catch this lunatic. He knew he couldn't be
~~~~~~~~~

held back by policies and procedures... especially since his intention was to find Summer, then kill the sonofabitch who took her.

~~~~~~~~~

Steve Layton had heard the voice message from Marcus. He immediately called him back. Marcus told him about the picture and the writing on the back. He also told him about his conversation with the club's owner.

The brothers drove to Diamonds Nightclub around 3:00pm. They were going there to have a heart to heart with the owner... Layton style.

When they arrived, they knocked on the front doors, but no one answered. Sean grabbed the handle of the door and pulled it open. As they entered, they couldn't see much of anything, at first, while their eyes adjusted to the dark club. The club wasn't open for business yet and no one appeared to be inside. Steve removed his 9mm from its holster and pointed down the left side of the main dance room, indicating for his brother to walk that way. He went to the right. Sean also removed his gun as he walked down the left side of the center stage. Suddenly, the laser lights overhead came on and the discothèque ball began to spin. The two brothers
~~~~~~~~~

stopped in their tracks and looked across the stage at each other. Just then, Type O Negative's - 'Summer Breeze' started to play loudly through the speakers. Sean started to feel nervous as he quickly panned the room. He spotted a dark haired woman lying in the center of the stage. She was obviously alive. He began to approach her. Steve immediately looked to the DJ booth but couldn't see anyone through the smokey glass. He gave his brother a signal to remain still, while he turned and approached the booth with his gun pointed at the small swinging door that led into it. He climbed the few steps up to the door and quickly flung it open. There was no one inside.

Just then a gunshot rang out. Steve turned from the top of the steps and saw his brother fall to the ground.

"Sean!" he screamed in panic as he raced down the steps and across the room, returning fire at a shadowy figure at the back of the stage. As he ran, he heard another gunshot and felt a burning sensation in his right shoulder as he fell over two leather chairs by the stage. He hit the ground with such force, he dropped his pistol. It slid away from him and out of sight.

He looked up just in time to clearly see a blonde woman with a gun, slipping out through the mirrored door at the back of the stage.

He turned his attention back to his brother, "Sean!" he yelled again, but there was no response. He could see his brother lying face down about ten feet from him, "Oh, Jesus Christ. Oh my God," he cried out as he attempted to crawl to his brother, "Sean! Jesus Christ Sean! Answer me goddamnit. Answer me!"

~ **43** ~

A woman staggered into Saint Stephens Hospital about 3:30pm. She was bleeding profusely from her stomach. Her face was ghostly white and sweat filled her medium length blonde hair. She had been shot once in the gut.

A nurse immediately came to her aid. She hollered for assistance as she caught the woman in her arms and fell to the ground. The Emergency Room was deserted, except for a man standing in the center of the waiting area with an oxygen mask strapped to his face. He was about 5' 8" tall, with a beer gut, reddish-brown hair, and a balding crown. His face showed evidence of a small goatee as he stared intently at the woman. All of a sudden the room filled with the sound of Genesis's - '*Mama*'. It gradually got louder over the hospital's speakers, as two other nurses and a doctor scurried into the room. They all stopped and stared in astonishment at the man with the oxygen mask.

The woman with the hole in her stomach opened her eyes wide, as the man removed the oxygen mask from his face. She immediately recognized him, as the man spread his arms out wide to his sides and threw his head back. The Emergency room doors flung open and a raging wind suddenly swept through the room. Everyone in the room remained in a trance as minutes ticked by to the eerie music.

The terrified nurse, who had originally come to the woman's aid, turned and asked the bleeding woman, "Who are you people?"

The woman closed her eyes slowly, took a deep breath through her nose, then reopened them as she responded, "We are The Beginning and The End." The woman then took a last breath, and died.

When the nurse looked back up at the man. He was gone. The wind immediately died and the music stopped.

~ 44 ~

The television above the bar was tuned to the Channel 7 News At Six. A breaking story came over the air. Darcel Grimes delivered the news in her usual monotone voice, "We've just received notice that the Satin Slasher has been shot... Yes...," she continued, as she held one hand up to the earpiece in her left ear, and looked away from the lead camera, "The reign of terror appears to be over here in Asheville... A Detective has shot the Satin Slasher... No more details are known at this time, but we'll have a complete update at ten." She turned back to face the lead camera, "In other news, District Attorney, Allen Morris has been picked up at the Asheville Airport, with a kilo of cocaine in his luggage..."

The sound of the TV was drowned out by the clanking together of beer mugs and a lot of hooting and hollering. It was Detective Steve Layton, celebrating the end of the tyrannical reign of terror Darcel Grimes had just spoken of.

The shooting had actually taken place almost four hours earlier, but had been concealed from the press, for good reason, until just now. The Detective was there at O'Neill's Bar and Grill with a dozen other cops, to celebrate the killing of the notorious slasher in the 'Slice-em' Dice-em' case. The two month reign of terror had finally come to an end, with the rescue of Summer Stevenson, the latest kidnapped victim, rescued unharmed, and the shooting of the psychopath who struck unbridled panic into the lives of women in the mountains of Western North Carolina.

"So, Steve... How did you know who the slasher was, and where to find the psycho and the Club owner's daughter?" one of the uniformed cops asked, as he slammed a whiskey sour.

"Well, to answer the *who* part of the question... It was merely a process of elimination. The whole world was a suspect, and I just narrowed it down," Layton answered in an overdramatized Hercule Poirot voice.

"Very funny," the cop replied.

Another plain clothed policeman asked, "You mean to say that it wasn't forensic evidence, fingerprints, hair samples, semen or skin under the fingernails?"

"No, actually, to begin with, none of the victims in this case were raped... Secondly, there was virtually no forensic evidence to be found at any of the crime scenes," Layton explained.

The faces of every cop in the room were staring at the Detective in awe and disbelief.

"So this case was solved on a hunch?"

"Not exactly... It was a bit more than a hunch. I had an informant working for me, who led me to the slasher's identity. I knew it was a game for the slasher and that it would have to end where it began... at Diamonds. But all that matters now is that we got the sick sonofabitch, and she's got a nice hole in her gut... courtesy of *yours truly*." Layton couldn't help but to smile. He wasn't exactly proud of actually shooting the woman. It was more a feeling of elation. He was just glad that it was all finally over. This case had pushed him to his limits, not only physically, but mentally, too.

"Woman?" one of the other officers asked, "It was a woman?"

Everyone in the room was also dumbfounded to hear this as well.

"Yes, it was actually one of my girlfriends from high school," Layton explained as the crowd listened intently, "She had held resentment towards me all these years, for our breakup. I'm not really sure why, but I speculate that it had something to do with my wife, Debbie. She always acted weird towards Debbie and me after we started dating, but I never could have imagined she was harboring such evilness for all these years.”

“So, I heard she had something to do with your wife’s death. Is this true?”

“Again, it is only speculation, but yes, I believe she was responsible for her death,” Layton answered.

“That’s fucking unreal!” another officer replied.

“I know. It was a shocker to me too. All those years of bitterness and resentment she held inside.” Layton looked down at the ground, as the sadness of his family’s deaths came flooding back to his mind. He forced himself to hold back the tears and changed his tone, “Obviously she was a twisted woman, but it’s over now... so, let’s celebrate!” Layton raised his beer in a toast. There was a lot more to this case than anyone else knew. It wasn’t really over, and Detective Layton knew it. This hadn’t been a lone deranged woman stalking and mutilating those poor dancers. It had been a team effort. The woman had only been the beginning. Now, he would have to find **the end**. . .

Other Books By Cash Pawley

Pray for Mercy
(Book 2 – The Pray Series)

Pray for Sight
(Book 3 – The Pray Series)

Unorthodox Angel

Betrayal

T.P.R.

www.ingramcontent.com/pod-product-compliance
Lightning Source LLC
Chambersburg PA
CBHW020737020826
48980CB00018B/561/J